No Hill to Die On

Peter Brandt Mysteries #4

Martin Roy Hill

No Hill to Die On

Published by

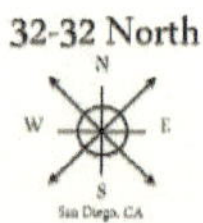

An imprint of

M. R. Hill Publishing

San Diego, California

For information contact:

www.martinroyhill.com

ISBN 979-8218575700

LCCN: 2024926694

Cover Design: RebecaCovers

Books by Martin Roy Hill

Fiction

The Linus Schag, NCIS, Thrillers
The Killing Depths (2012)
The Butcher's Bill (2017)
Upriver (2022)

The Peter Brandt Mysteries
Empty Places (2013)
The Last Refuge (2016)
The Fourth Rising (2020)

The USCG DSF-Papa Thrillers
Polar Melt: A Novel (2019)
Chimera Island (2021)

Standalones
Duty: Stories of Mystery and Suspense from the Cold War and Beyond (2012)
Eden: A Sci-Fi Novella (2014)
Codename: Parsifal (2023)

Nonfiction
War Stories: Tales of Leadership, Courage, Blunders, and SNAFUs (2018)

Dedication

For Harvey
KIA
Vietnam
1966
My inspiration for Keith Brandt.

Prologue

Saigon
1972

THE CLUB DID NOT differ from hundreds of other Saigon clubs that catered to U.S. servicemen during the war. Dimly lit, crowded with tables, and smelling of marijuana and hashish, the room offered cheap drinks, the ear-blasting wail of western rock music, and a dozen young, sensuous dark-skinned girls with almond eyes swaying to the beat. But unlike the years before, American servicemen didn't crowd the club and most of the tables stood empty.

Most of the non-indigenous forces began withdrawing from the war the previous year, handing responsibility for the fight to the South Vietnamese. The American presence was a mere shadow of what it had been at the height of the war. Were it not for North Vietnam's Easter Offensive, the two American Marines sitting at a corner table—a sergeant and a private—would not have been there. The two were members of a battalion of Marines airlifted in from offshore amphibious landing ships to provide security at the Da Nang airbase, which was again filling up with U.S. planes helping to stave off the north's invasion.

The sergeant finished his beer, wiped foam from his mouth with the back of his hand and yawned.

"Let's blow this place," he said. "There's got to be someplace with more action."

The private shook his head. "I like it here," he said. He gave a wolfish grin as he leered at a bar girl a few feet away. The girl smiled back and did a little pirouette to show off the curves underneath her tight *ao dai* dress. "You go on. I'll catch up later at the hotel. I got a little business transaction to do."

"You better watch out," the sergeant said, "or you're going to get the clap from that business."

The private's eyes never left the girl. He downed the remains of his beer and stood with a slight sway. "Said I'd catch up later, man."

He stumbled toward the girl and his friend walked toward the door. The sergeant glanced back from the door and saw the girl wrap her arms around the private's neck and press her body against his.

The sergeant shook his head and left the bar. He had taken only a dozen steps when a blast threw him to the ground. Shaking his head, the sergeant raised himself and looked back. Smoke bellowed from the club's blown-out windows. He staggered to his feet and half stumbled, half ran back into the club.

Then the world exploded again.

Chapter 1

San Diego, California
1997

SHAKESPEARE BELIEVED THE PAST is prologue. But most times we hope the past is just the past, something that happened, perhaps inevitably, and then is gone and forgotten. Unfortunately, the past has a nasty habit of rearing up again when you least expect it—or want it. Take ghosts, for instance. Not the kind that haunt buildings, but the kind that haunt your dreams. I know all about those ghosts.

But the past I slammed up against that day wasn't my own. It was my older brother Keith's. My dead brother Keith.

It came as a phone call from Rhonda, Keith's fiancée. Former fiancée. I hadn't heard from her in over twenty years, since my family buried Keith with full military honors after he was killed in Vietnam in the waning days of the war. Some ghosts refuse to stay buried.

"Hello, Peter?" Despite the years, I recognized the voice. It was a little deeper, a little rougher, but it was hers. "It's Rhonda."

"I know," I said.

"Oh?" She paused and cleared her throat. "Well, how are you?"

"Fine."

"It's been a long time, hasn't it?" she said.

"Twenty-five years," I said.

"Yes, well …"

She hesitated again. I could tell she was nervous. It's difficult to revisit the past, especially when you haven't looked at it for so long. I sighed and tried to be nicer.

"How are you doing, Rhonda?" I asked.

"Oh …" She seemed taken aback by my question. "Oh, I'm fine. You know … I read one of your books and, uh, I'm in town on business. I thought I'd look you up. Thought maybe we could get together. Get some coffee or something?"

Now I hesitated. I'm not one to go pounding on the door of things past. Well, yes, I am. But I was trying to change.

"Look, Peter," Rhonda said. "I *need* to talk to you. About Keith's death."

"That was a long time ago, Rhonda. Time we let sleeping dogs lie." I wondered to myself how many more clichés about the past I could remember.

"No, this is something new," she said. "Something wrong, really—about how the Marines said Keith was killed."

Something in my throat hardened. I swallowed, but it wouldn't go down. "What do you mean, Rhonda?"

"Peter, I need to meet you in person," she insisted. "There's something I need to show you."

Something in her voice told me I should meet with her. Then a little voice in the back of my head also told me I should meet her. I could've sworn it was Keith's voice.

"Okay," I said. "Where are you staying?"

Rhonda gave me the name of a hotel on Harbor Island in San Diego Bay. "I'll meet you in the restaurant."

"Give me an hour," I told her, and hung up.

"Rhonda? You're meeting another woman in a hotel?"

Jo Rice grinned at me from the couch where she sat with Jack, my oversized orange long-haired tabby, curled in her lap. I explained who Rhonda was and what she said.

"I sensed some tension on your end," Jo said.

Jo—short for Joanne—was former military police and now a security consultant. She had the instincts of a New

York homicide detective. She also had short blonde hair, an adorable, crooked smile that always melted my iron heart, and a tall, lithesome body that was just short of perfection. The lapse in perfection was because of an ugly scar that marred her right thigh, a wound received during Operation Desert Storm when a friendly fire incident wiped out her small MP unit.

"Rhonda was like an older sister to me," I said. "After we buried Keith, we all promised to stay in touch, but we never saw her again after the funeral. My parents tried to explain that she needed to move on, but for ten-year-old me, it was like losing a brother *and* a sister."

"A little self-indulgent wouldn't you say?" Jo said.

Jo not only had a New York cop's instincts, she could be as hard-nosed as one, a trait that earned her the nickname "Cold as Ice Rice."

"Hey, I was only ten," I whined. "You want to come?"

She looked down at Jack and gave his long, marmalade fur a ruffle. "What, and disturb his royal highness's nap?"

I laughed, gave Jo a peck on the forehead, scratched Jack's ear, and left.

As I walked into the hotel's restaurant, I scanned the tables for a familiar face. I didn't see one. Twenty-five years is a long time, and people change. The memories we keep of them are ghosts shimmering in the dark, like specters of our memories.

I was ten when Keith was killed. He was nineteen. There were no other siblings before, after, or in between us. Yes, my birth was an accident, something Keith never let me forget as we were growing up. Yet, he was a good big brother, and like a lot of younger brothers, I idolized him. Rhonda was a year younger than Keith. They met in high school and became engaged soon after Keith completed his basic training. She was a willowy brunette with happy, twinkling eyes, a perfect smile and contagious laugh, and a sweetness that was neither cloying nor made up. She became a member of our family, and I considered her my big sister.

A woman stood up from her table and looked at me. "Peter?"

Keith would forever remain young, but his former fiancée would not. Twenty-five years later, Rhonda White was heavier, her face rounder, her eyes dulled with life and disappointment, her smile forced. I got the immediate impression she rarely laughed anymore. The teenage girl I knew was as dead as my brother.

But then, I wasn't that ten-year-old boy anymore.

I nodded and approached her. "Rhonda?"

"Peter!" She waved me over and held out her hand as I neared. I took the hand, but she took it away. "Oh, what are we doing?" Instead of shaking my hand, she hugged me.

A waitress came, and we ordered coffee. Then Rhonda looked me over and said, "I don't think I would have recognized you if I hadn't read your book and saw your picture on the back cover. Look at you, you're all grown up."

"Well, there are some people who would debate that," I said.

"How are your parents?" Rhonda asked.

I looked away for a moment and when I turned back, her face showed she already had guessed the answer.

"They're both gone," I said.

She touched my hand. "Oh, Peter, I'm so sorry."

I simply nodded.

"You know I loved your parents," Rhonda said.

"They loved you, too," I said. I didn't think it worth mentioning so had I.

"Maybe, but …" She looked away and said, "I'm sorry I stayed away from all of you. Your folks tried to call me and write to me, but …"

"Look, Rhonda," I said, "none of us blame you for not wanting to see us, to be reminded …"

"Oh, Peter, losing Keith hurt so much," she said. "Every time I thought about it … I—I had to put it behind me …"

I reached out and touched her hand. "We all had to put it behind us."

"I used to wonder what my life would have been like if he lived … if we got married like we planned …" She sniffed, took a handkerchief from her purse, and dabbed her eyes.

"Look, Rhonda, even if Keith hadn't died, you two probably might not have gotten married anyway," I said. "If Keith came home, he might have been a totally different guy and not someone you could love anymore. War changes a person. You said you read one of my books, so you should understand that."

Rhonda gave me a sad smile and nodded. She reached over and ran a finger along the scar on my face. "It changed you, didn't it?"

"You're damn right it did," I answered.

For most of my adult life I have been a journalist. I started out covering crime in the California desert, then along the U.S.-Mexican border. Eventually, I worked my way south to cover Ronald Reagan's illegal wars in Central America, where a Salvadoran soldier slammed his rifle butt into my head, leaving me with chronic headaches and a scar running from my forehead down over my left eye. I also covered Operation Desert Storm, the war that left Jo with a limp and the rest of her MP team dead. War changes everything.

Rhonda sat staring at me for a while, then sighed. "I think I could use a drink." She waved the waitress over and ordered a glass of wine. I ordered scotch. While we waited for the drinks, she asked, "Well, besides writing about wars, what else have you been up to? Do you have a wife and family?"

I shook my head. "Divorced," I said. I didn't bother telling her my ex-wife was also dead, murdered by a corrupt cop. "You?"

"Divorced." She gave another sad smile. "Twice. No kids."

The drinks came, and we each took long sips. Then I asked, "Okay, Rhonda. So, what is this news about Keith you wanted to tell me?"

She seemed to shrink into herself. For the first time, I saw the old Rhonda again—not from the happy high school days, but from the day of Keith's funeral. The young, scared, and troubled girl with hollow, tear-reddened eyes staring at the future she would no longer have.

"I—um …" She pulled a tissue from her purse and wiped a tear from her eye. "I'm … I'm not sure Keith is dead."

Without thinking, I slammed my hand on the table and barked, "What? How can you say that?"

She jumped when I slammed the table, but quickly gathered herself. I looked around and saw other customers staring at me. "I'm sorry," I told her, and I was. "But how can you say that?"

"Because the man who supposedly died with him," she said, "isn't dead."

Chapter 2

RHONDA PULLED A COMPANY brochure from her purse, opened it, and laid it on the table. She tapped a long, polished fingernail on a photograph of a man. "Do you know him?"

The photo showed a portrait of a middle-aged man with a thin, horse-like face and a prominent nose that followed the contours of his face. A thin pimp's mustache angled down from his nose, stopping at the corners of a mouth with equally thin lips bearing a con man's smile. The eyes were dark and lifeless—shark eyes. The caption below the photograph identified him as Thomas Danner.

I shook my head. "Who is he?"

"He's a local businessman I've been meeting with," Rhonda said. "Let me back up and explain something. I work for a technology solutions company. I'm in sales. We provide companies with computers, servers, and software solutions. All for civilian use. But a lot of what we sell is called 'dual-use' technology, meaning it can also have military applications and can't be exported. Because of that, we limit our sales to U.S. companies. But, in truth, once the technology is out of our hands, we're not really concerned where it ends up or with whom."

"Ah, American capitalism," I sneered. "Is this a great country or what?"

"A girl's got to make a living, Peter," Rhonda said.

I nodded. "Go on. So, who's this Danner guy?"

"He calls himself a technology consultant," Rhonda said, "though I don't think he knows a thing about software or hardware. I think he's just acting as a middleman."

"A middleman for whom?"

She shrugged. "Who knows? Like I said, we're not real persnickety about things like that. Once we have our end-use papers, we wash our hands of it. It's somebody else's concern." Rhonda gave her head a shake and waved the question away. "Anyway, we're digressing, Peter. I just wanted to explain why I was here in San Diego and how I met this man Danner." Her fingers made air quotes as she said his name.

"Okay."

She reached into her purse again and placed a black-and-white Polaroid photo on the table between us. The picture showed three young people, two men—boys, really—with Marine Corps high-and-tight haircuts and a pretty girl. The girl was Rhonda, twenty-five years younger. One boy was Keith. The other one I didn't know, but he looked eerily similar to the middle-aged man in the brochure photo. His hair was shorter, but he had the same horse face and nose, the same cheesy mustache, the same fake smile, the same dead eyes.

Rhonda tapped the unknown boy's face. "This is Tommy, Tommy Dykstra. Everyone called him TD. He was Keith's best friend in the Marines. They went through boot camp and infantry training together and were in the same platoon when they went overseas."

She picked up the photo and studied it with a sad smile. "They were inseparable. A little too inseparable for my taste."

"You didn't like him, this TD guy?" I asked.

"Well, he made it difficult for Keith and me to get some time alone so we could …" She waved the image away. "Well, you know. But, no, I really didn't care for him much, I guess. He was always so … cocky. I don't mean in an I'm-a-big-bad-Marine way. He seemed to think he could do anything he wanted and get away with it. The prick even made a move on me once, but I never told Keith that."

"He doesn't sound like the kind of guy Keith would care for," I said.

"Keith said boot camp was tough and the only way to get through it was to have a good buddy watching your back," Rhonda said. "And I think Keith thought he needed to take care of TD. You know what he was like."

"Like the way he always took care of me," I said, nodding. "I admit the kid in this photo has a resemblance to this Danner guy, but a lot of people look alike."

"That's what I thought when I first met Danner," Rhonda said. "But TD had this tic on the right side of his mouth. Whenever he got nervous, it would show up."

"And this guy Danner has the same tic?" I guessed.

"The exact same tic," she said, nodding. "The first time it showed up was when my colleagues and I were introduced to him. As soon as he heard my name, his mouth twitched."

"He recognized you?"

Rhonda shrugged. "Let's be real, Peter. After twenty-five years I'm not the skinny little girl I was," she said. "I think he recognized my name. After two divorces, I went back to using my maiden name, White."

"Did he say anything about knowing you or someone with the same name?"

"No," Rhonda said. "And at first, I didn't recognize him. But when we started talking about the end use for the stuff we were selling him, his mouth started twitching and I remembered TD. Everything came flooding back to me. I had to run to the restroom and compose myself. And that was when I remembered something else."

Rhonda sipped her wine before continuing.

"While we were waiting in his office lobby for our meeting, I saw Danner—I didn't know who he was at that point—but I saw him leave the men's room. He was rolling down his shirt sleeves, and I caught a glance of a tattoo on his lower right arm. A Marine Corps anchor and globe."

"The same tattoo Keith had on his lower right arm," I said.

Rhonda nodded. "TD, too," she said. "They got them at the same time after finishing boot camp."

I swirled the photo of Keith, Rhonda, and TD around with my finger, so it faced me again. There was a definite physical similarity between TD and this guy Danner. Everyone is said to have a doppelgänger, a near twin. There has to be a limited number of genes in our gene pool. Mix them together over a millennium, and you're bound to come with almost exact human duplicates. After all, the human DNA pool isn't all that deep. Ask any recipient of the Darwin Award. Oh, wait, you can't ask them. They're all dead, a result of their own folly.

But when you add together the resemblance, the same facial tic, the same tattoo in the same place, and not only the same initials but the same given name, you have to be dealing with something more than genetic roulette.

"Okay, Rhonda," I said, "you've made your point. For the sake of argument, let's say this guy Danner is the same person as this TD you and Keith hung out with. So what? People change their names all the time for all kinds of reasons. Maybe this TD came home from the war and changed his name to distance himself from it."

Rhonda was shaking her head before I even finished my sentence.

"No, no, no, Peter," she said. "Keith and TD were killed the same day in the same battle." She tapped the table with a fingernail for emphasis as she spoke. "Do you remember what Keith's medal citation said?"

"Of course," I said.

The Marines posthumously awarded the Silver Star to Keith for heroism on the day he died. The citation said he was involved in a battle with North Vietnamese troops around the airbase at Da Nang when he raced out under fire to rescue a wounded Marine. A mortar round landed nearby, killing them instantly.

"The Marine Keith was trying to save when he was killed was TD," Rhonda said. "There's a new website; it's called The Virtual Vietnam Wall. Like the real Vietnam Wall in DC, it lists the names of everyone killed in the war by date. TD's name is right next to Keith's."

"Okay." I drew out the word as the rusty little gears in my head tried to make sense of what she was saying. Or perhaps they were moving slowly because I really didn't want to come to the conclusion I suspected she had already reached.

"Keith had a closed casket burial," she whispered.

There it was. The damage to Keith's body from the blast was too severe to repair with mortician's wax and makeup. At least, that's what the Marines told us. We were never able to lay eyes on him. If TD's body were as mangled as Keith's, he too would have had a closed casket. It's possible only pieces of Keith's and TD's remains were recovered, hence the closed coffins. That happens a lot in war. But it's also possible TD's coffin was empty or had someone else's body in it.

And if TD didn't die in Vietnam and was living today under an assumed name, then maybe—just maybe—Keith, too, was still alive.

I threw back the last of my scotch and ordered another. This time, I made it a double.

Chapter 3

I FOLLOWED THAT SCOTCH with another when I got home. Except for Jack, the bungalow was empty. Jo left a note saying she was called back to her office to "put out another fire." Jack seemed to sense my mood. As I sat at my computer, he leapt onto my lap and purred while kneading my thighs. Jo called it "making biscuits." I called it painful.

By no means was I convinced Rhonda was right about Danner being TD. All she had was one coincidence piled on another. But there is an old mob saying I heard when I was covering crime as a reporter—or maybe I read it in a James Bond novel. It goes: "Once is happenstance. Twice is coincidence. Three times is enemy action." Still, we had no actual proof of who Danner was. Despite the opinion of many corrupt politicians and their gullible constituents, journalists really do rely on facts for their stories. At least the good ones do.

Waking up my computer, I searched the internet for Thomas Danner. I used several variations of his name—Tom Danner, Tommy Danner, T. Danner, Tomas Danner-nose—I couldn't get that schnoz out of my head. After running those searches, I came up with practically nothing on the man. That raised my suspicions. Businesspeople like publicity. They enjoy being seen and heard. Many executives hired PR firms to brag to the world about their accomplishments. Unfortunately, as they rise through the corporate hierarchy, they start believing their own hype. There was some clown in New York named Trump who claimed to be the richest man in the world despite having declared bankruptcy half a dozen times and losing money on a casino he owned. He was even talking about making a run for the White House.

I found only one web page with any information on Danner's firm, Danner Consulting, little more than an HTML version of the company brochure Rhonda had shown me. It claimed Danner's experience in Asia made the company one of the top international import-export consulting firms. "Thomas Danner," it said, "accumulated twenty years of experience in the import-export business working in the Far East, including Thailand, Hong Kong, China, and Vietnam before returning to the U.S."

Do people still refer to Asia as the Far East?

Danner's last claim had to be a recent development, since President Bill Clinton had restored relations with Vietnam only two years before. That meant he had only recently returned to the States. I made a note to check the city and county records for a business license and DBA record.

I stopped my reading as my mind wandered. Restoring relations with a country we had been at war with always raised strained emotions in the veterans who fought there and the families who lost loved ones there. Washington claimed we were fighting in Vietnam to prevent the spread of communism. If South Vietnam fell to the North, they said, communism would spread across the land like a string of dominoes falling one after another. The South lost, but twenty-five years later, the dominoes still hadn't fallen. Yes, Vietnam was communist, but American businesses were still eager to trade with them. The Vietnam Wall in Washington had fifty-eight thousand names on it. I was sure Australia and New Zealand and the other allies who fought there with us had similar monuments. God only knows how many Vietnamese, both North and South, died.

I sighed, shook my head, and continued reading.

Danner's page touted several recommendations from companies he'd done business with. Most of them had Asian names. I searched the internet for each company. The only one that struck gold was a Taiwanese firm that produced fortune cookies for export to the U.S. I continued my search for another hour with no results. Jack jumped off my lap, sashayed into the kitchen, and gave a plaintive meow to let me know it was dinner time.

Jo returned shortly after, carrying a paper bag. The fragrance of Chinese cooking filled the bungalow. Jack deserted his dinner, trotted up to Jo, and wrapped himself around her legs. "Oh, you poor little boy," she cooed. "Hasn't your daddy fed you yet?"

"Like hell I haven't," I grumbled and hooked a thumb toward the half-full cat bowl. "What did you get?"

"Kung pao chicken, mushu pork, spring rolls, and rice," she said.

Neither of us were big on cooking. Chinese food was our go-to source for sustenance. Jack loved Chinese food.

"Put some of the pork on top of his food," I said.

Jo did, and soon the small kitchen resounded with Jack's purring.

"So, how'd it go with your brother's fiancée?" Jo asked as she emptied the contents of the bag onto the kitchen table.

I laid out plates and utensils—nothing I had qualified as silverware—and briefed Jo on what Rhonda told me.

"Do you believe her?" Jo asked when I finished.

I placed a bottle of wine on the table, along with two glasses, and shrugged. "I don't know," I said. "A lot of coincidences, but—"

"No proof." Like I said, Jo had the instincts of a New York cop.

"Exactly." I spooned some kung pao over my rice and jammed a forkful into my mouth and chewed. "On the other hand, this guy Danner raises the hackles on my neck."

"You think he's hinky?"

"Very," I said. "I searched for him on the internet but got nada. His company web page looks like a child made it, and I didn't find anything that I could verify. He claims he worked in Asia for some twenty years, but I didn't find anything to corroborate it. His page lists companies he's worked with, but I only found one company on the net and …" Looking down, I saw a fortune cookie on the table, picked it up, and examined it. "… and I think they made these." I shrugged and dropped the cookie back on the tabletop. "It's almost like he didn't exist until he returned to the U.S."

I wrapped some mushu into a thin pancake and took a bite.

"She's a very sad lady," I said after chewing and swallowing. "Keith was the love of her life. When she lost him, well … Two divorces, no children, a job she doesn't really care for with a company she admits is dishonest. So, she meets a guy who happens to look like this TD and that reminded her of Keith. Now she's grasping at straws, wanting to believe he's still alive and they can have the happy life she once dreamed of."

"Those are pretty flimsy straws," Jo said, then delicately placed a piece of chicken in her mouth with a pair of chopsticks.

I nodded. "But a drowning person will clutch at anything to stay alive," I said.

Jo didn't spend the night. She had an early morning meeting, so she returned to her new apartment that overlooked San Diego Bay. She had owned an expensive house in Rancho Santa Fe, but it was too large for one person. It also reminded her of her late husband, the man she had dumped me for some years before. They weren't good memories. The marriage wasn't good. Neither was the man.

Ours was a strange relationship. I met Jo not long after the Gulf War, where she received her leg wound. She was still an army captain in the MPs, and we were both investigating the friendly fire incident that had left the men under her command dead. We grew close, but Jo wanted commitment and I—having fouled up my marriage—was afraid of it. Several months ago, her husband was murdered. Jo came to me for help. Again, we grew close, and I realized I was ready to commit. But coming out of a bad marriage, she wasn't. We decided to take it day-by-day and remain what a recent Alanis Morissette song called "friends with bene-fits."

Jack pouted for a while after Jo left, but then curled up on the couch where she had been sitting and went to sleep. I sat in front of my computer and ran a search for the Virtual Vietnam Wall Rhonda had mentioned. It was a simple site, but one that offered multiple ways of looking up a lost loved one, and I found Keith's name with no problem. The real Vietnam Wall in DC has several panels. Listed on those panels are the names of those killed in order of the day they died. Keith's name was on the last panel among those who died in the waning months of the war. Right next to Keith's name was Tommy Dykstra's.

The Virtual Wall allowed me to read a brief copy of Keith's service record that included his birth date, death date, where he died, and how. The "how" listed "small arms fire." That was strange. Keith's Silver Star citation said he died from mortar fire. That was the reason for the closed-casket burial. I looked up TD's listing. It, too, listed small arms fire as the cause of death.

I printed out both lists. With the date and place of their deaths, I could look up more information about the battle they died in. Maybe then I could figure how my brother and his best friend died. *If* they really had died.

Chapter 4

THE NEXT MORNING, I rose early, fed Jack, then went for a run down to the beach. San Diego's Ocean Beach neighborhood was a throwback to the 1960s. Smoke shops, second-hand clothing stores, antique shops, and funky little cafés and eateries lined its streets. The little bungalow I rented was part of that era. Locals did their best to prevent the encroachment of chain restaurants, stores, and bars, and I thanked them for it.

It was early enough in the morning that the streets were still vacant, but as I ran along the esplanade, I encountered several fellow joggers. All were younger than I, many of them very attractive young women in tight short-shorts and tube tops or running bras. Now and then, one would smile my way or even wave as they passed me. Most ignored me.

Behind me, I heard a familiar voice call out, "Hey, Professor Pete."

I turned and Cindy Lawford trotted up to me. Cindy was a short but shapely twenty-something student of mine at the city college where I taught journalism part-time to supplement my income from book royalties and the occasional magazine assignment I received from a national news weekly. She had long, dark-brown hair and a smooth olive complexion, and wore running tights and a sports bra that left little to the imagination—not that I needed to imagine. One night, after too many drinks, we ended up back at my place. These days, however, we confined our relationship to the classroom and to the odd times Cindy would babysit Jack while I was away.

"Hey, Cindy," I greeted her. "What's up?"

"Just trying to wake up," she said, running in place to keep her heart rate up. I did my best to avoid staring at her heaving breasts, but it was hypnotic.

"Long night partying?"

"Long night working on that last assignment you gave us," she said.

"Good for you," I said. "So, I can expect it on time?"

"You bet," she replied, then looking at her wristwatch, added, "I gotta go. Got a class in an hour. Give Jack a hug."

She jogged away, leaving me feeling the same as I always did when I saw her around the neighborhood—old.

I did a few sprints on the beach, trying in vain to push back the years, then jogged home and showered. Jack danced around my legs, mewing as I fried some eggs, so when I finished, I tithed him his share and ate the rest while reading the paper. The local section had a short piece about a search of San Diego Bay for a reported suicide, and I cursed myself for reading it. I had spent so much of my journalism career covering death, I wanted nothing to do with it anymore—including reading about it.

After breakfast, I left Jack napping on the bed and drove the Mustang downtown to city hall. I avoided downtown as much as possible. Each time I drove its streets, I felt like a lab rat in a maze. Downtown San Diego was a labyrinth of crowded, narrow, one-way streets cast in the ever-present shadows of office and condominium high-rises crowded together like patrons in a standing-room-only theatrical production. Highly paid, well-dressed professionals walked shoulder-to-shoulder with shabbily dressed down-at-the-heels, many pushing their life's belongings in stolen grocery carts. Tourists in bright shirts and shorts gawked at them both as they rode through the streets in bicycle-drawn rickshaws.

It took me twenty minutes to get from my place to downtown, another thirty to find a parking place that didn't demand a small fortune and then walk to city hall. In the clerk's office, I looked up the business license for Danner

Consulting. It was listed as a sole proprietorship operating in the technology field. The sole proprietor was Thomas Danner. The license was less than two years old, so he hadn't been in town long.

I walked the few blocks to the local chamber of commerce and checked their directory of businesses for Danner Consulting. There was no listing. I asked a secretary if anyone in the office had heard of Danner Consulting. After asking around, she came back shaking her head. Thanking her, I left the building and made my way back to my car.

It puzzled me why the chamber had no listing or knowledge of Danner Consulting. For anyone setting up a new business in a city, the first stop would be the local chamber of commerce. It was there they could make contacts and network with potential clients. Not associating with the chamber was like flying blind.

Or, maybe, flying stealth.

Retrieving the Mustang, I drove north on the I-5 past the turnoff for Ocean Beach and headed for La Jolla's UCSD college campus to use its library. I could have used the public library while I was downtown, but for too long now it had become a second home to the downtown homeless. Perhaps, I should say their only home.

The UCSD library, with its modern cantilever architecture, squatted in the center of the campus like an alien spaceship. Each time I saw it, I marveled at the fact that the concrete arms extending out diagonally from its base could bear so much weight, especially in a region prone to earthquakes. As I did each time before entering, I said a quiet prayer asking there be no earthquakes while I was inside.

Using the information gleaned from their Virtual Wall entries, I used the library's microfiche newspaper archive to look up any news stories about the battle in which Keith and TD had died. There wasn't much. With the withdrawal ongoing, interest in Vietnam had dwindled even among the news media. A few wrap-up stories mentioned an attack on the airfield at Da Nang and that a battalion of Marines beat it back. Casualties were described as "light." Most of the reports were about the difficulty the Army of the Republic of Vietnam—ARVN—was having holding back the communist onslaught. It was a subliminal message saying the war was lost and we should get the hell out of it *now*. One small story mentioned renewed bombing by Viet Cong insurgents in Saigon itself, including one that killed two U.S. Navy investigators.

I had better luck in the bookstacks. The Marine Corps had produced several histories on the last months of the war, and one of them was about the fighting around Da Nang airfield. Written by a Marine Corps historian, it contained detailed maps, timelines, and personal accounts of the battle. The narration included each minute of the fighting, the position of friendly and enemy troops, and accounts of each person wounded or killed.

Except for Keith and TD.

I read through the report again, more slowly this time, in case I had missed something. Still, no mention of Keith or TD. There was a casualty list at the back of the report with the names listed in alphabetical order. Both Keith and TD were listed as KIA—killed in action. I checked the index for the names of those listed as casualties. Each Marine on the casualty list was also in the index with the page number or numbers where they were mentioned—except Keith and TD.

I leaned back in my chair and puzzled over that omission. If two of your Marines were blown to smithereens in a battle, I would think you'd include some mention of it in your history—especially if one of them received the Silver Star for his actions. So, why weren't Keith's and TD's deaths recorded in detail like the others? An oversight or an overt omission?

Pulling my reporter's notebook out, I started jotting down the names, ranks, and hometowns of the Marines mentioned. It would be like looking for the proverbial needle in a haystack, but I thought I might find someone who knew Keith and TD and could tell me what happened to them. The average Marine Corps battalion was between five and six hundred men strong. Fortunately, not every Marine involved was mentioned by name. Still, it took much of the afternoon for me to finish writing out the names and details like rank, unit, and squad. When I finished, my head ached and so did my hand.

But at least there hadn't been an earthquake. For that, I was thankful.

Chapter 5

I REALLY HADN'T DISCOVERED much, but I called Rhonda on my cell just to let her know I was following up on our discussion. Her hotel, however, said she was no longer registered there. The receptionist hesitated when I asked if she left any information on where I could reach her. She covered the mouthpiece of the phone and spoke to someone else at the reception desk. A moment later, she told me, "I'm sorry, sir, but we're not allowed to give out that kind of information," and hung up.

Rhonda had told me she would be in town a few more days. Perhaps her business dealings with Danner Consulting were cut short. If so, I would find a message from her waiting on my land line's answering machine.

When I got home, my answering machine showed I had several calls, but no one left a message. Jack pranced around the kitchen mewling, so I fed him dinner. As I poured myself a scotch, the phone rang. I picked it up.

"Brandt."

"Pete, this is Mike McCarty."

"Hey, Moondoggie! Cowabunga!" Lieutenant Mike McCarty was a homicide investigator with the San Diego Police Department. He was also a world-class competitive surfer. Whenever we talked, I couldn't resist throwing every 1950s-Sandra-Dee-as-Gidget cliché I could at him. "Surf's up, dude. Hang ten."

I could hear McCarty sigh at the other end.

"How the hell would I know if the surf is up?" he said. "I spent half the night dragging San Diego Harbor for a body."

"Gnarly," I said.

Mike sighed again. "Do you know a woman named Rhonda White?"

My heart stopped. McCarty never asked a question like that unless something had happened to the person.

"Yeah," I croaked out. "She's an old family friend. What happened, Mike?"

"Hers is the body we dragged the bay for," Mike said. "I need to talk to you ASAP. In my office."

Mike McCarty didn't make requests. There was no other answer. "I'm on my way," I said.

When I first worked in San Diego for a wire service, SDPD's headquarters were in a low-slung Spanish-style building reminiscent of one of the old missions built along the Camino Real—the King's Highway. The department's new headquarters were in a modern five-story office edifice that had none of the appeal of the old headquarters, but it was bright, roomy, and air-conditioned.

I grabbed the lanyard with my police press credentials from the glove box and dropped it over my head as I entered the station. The last time I'd been there, an attractive brunette officer had signed me in and let me through the security door. The entire time, she never smiled. This time, an oversized and distinctly unattractive male sergeant buzzed me into the department's inner sanctum. He also never smiled.

Most police officials decorated their walls and bookshelves with departmental awards or photos of various political luminaries. Mike's bookshelves carried surfing trophies from around the world, and photos of him on foreign shores surrounded by bikini-clad beauties. A surfboard stood in one corner. Mike himself was in his late thirties, still fit and trim, with light-brown hair and moustache, both bleached by the sun. He waved me into his office with a sour look on his face. I decided not to redo my Gidget schtick. Neither of us was in the mood.

I sat in his guest chair like a sack of potatoes. "What happened, Mike?"

McCarty glanced at his computer screen, then rubbed his eyes. They were red and swollen, and not from sea spray. He replied to my question with all the emotion of a printed police report. Just the facts, ma'am.

"Dispatch received a 9-1-1 call yesterday morning reporting that some joggers saw what they thought was a woman's body in the water off Harbor Island," he said. "A Harbor Police patrol car was dispatched as well as a Harbor Police boat. They found nothing and were about to cancel the call when another good Samaritan called in saying they found a woman's handbag and shoes on the Harbor Island shoreline. They belonged to a Rhonda White, who turned out to be a guest at the hotel. We also found her rental car parked near where the shoes and purse were found.

"After that, we took over and launched a full-body recovery operation—our officers scoured the harbor shoreline, while the Harbor Police and Coast Guard searched the bay waters. Last night, the Harbor Police started dragging the seabed around Harbor Island. This morning, a boat owner discovered a body of a woman floating in the Harbor Island Marina."

When he finished, Mike yawned, stood, and poured himself a cup of black java from a coffee maker on a small counter. He didn't bother offering me one.

"We got a list of all the phone calls she made from her room," he continued as he sat down again. "There was only one local call—to you. So, tell me again how you know this woman."

I explained how Rhonda had been Keith's fiancée when he died in Vietnam.

"Huh," he said when I finished. "Your brother was a Marine?" I nodded. He looked at me and shook his head. "So, what happened with you?"

It was my turn to sigh. "Every family has a black sheep," I said.

"Some blacker than others," McCarty muttered.

I took no offense. Just as I joked about Mike being a surfer, he chided me about being a reporter. He really wasn't a bad fellow—for a cop.

"And you hadn't seen her in how long?" Mike asked.

"Since we buried Keith," I replied. "About twenty-five years ago."

"And after all this time, she just called you up out of the blue to say hello?"

"Not quite," I said. "She wanted to tell me something."

"About what?"

"About his death."

McCarty eyed me closely. "Twenty-five years after the fact?"

"She was in town on business and met someone who looked familiar," I said. "She thought he looked like a middle-aged version of my brother's best friend in the Marines. They were both reported killed at the same time during the same battle."

"And she called you up to what? Reminisce?"

I filled Mike in on Thomas Danner, the old photo of Keith, Rhonda, and TD, the similar nervous tic, and the Marine Corps tattoo. When I finished, Mike sat back, used his right thumb and forefinger to smooth his mustache, and regarded me through hooded eyes.

"So, with this cheerful little … homecoming, what was her mental state like?" he asked.

"Her what?"

"Did she seem depressed?" He shrugged. "Maybe suicidal?"

The ends of my mouth tugged down as I considered the question. I shook my head. "No," I said. "I don't think so. If she was, she hid it well. She was twice divorced, no kids, and not happy in her job, but she didn't act suicidal. In some way, she was just the opposite. I think she believed that if this Danner guy *was* TD, then maybe Keith was still alive, too."

Mike's mustache imitated my frown as he regarded me with a somber nod.

"Good," he said.

"Good?"

He nodded again. "If you had tried to convince me she was suicidal, you would have become my number one suspect."

"Suspect?" I said.

"Drowning victims don't usually float," McCarty said. "When someone drowns, they expel all the air from their lungs. Without their lungs full of air, they sink, and they don't come back up until days or weeks later when decomp gasses make their bodies buoyant again."

"You're say—"

"Rhonda White was murdered," McCarty said.

Chapter 6

"WE WON'T KNOW FOR certain until we get the coroner's report, but it looks like she was choked before she was put into the bay," Mike said. "There was bruising around the neck. It's possible whoever did this applied enough pressure to collapse her trachea, trapping air in her lungs."

"Making her buoyant," I muttered.

Mike nodded. "Tell me about this Danner, the guy she thought was your brother's friend."

"He has some kind of technology consulting business," I said. "His website claims he spent the past twenty-some years importing and exporting technology throughout Asia."

"Claims?" Mike asked.

"There were the names of supposed client companies. I tried looking them up on the internet, but couldn't find any companies with those names," I said. "Except one, and I don't think they would be a client of his."

"Why not?"

"They make fortune cookies, not computers," I said.

McCarty nodded and typed something into his computer. "Go on."

"I pulled his business license down at city hall," I continued. "It said he'd been in business here in San Diego for less than two years. The chamber of commerce never heard of him."

Some more typing, then, "Go on."

I shook my head. "That's about it, Mike," I said. "It's like this guy didn't exist until he showed up here two years ago."

"I'll check him out," McCarty said. "What about this friend of your brother's, TD. Are you sure he was killed, too?"

"Both their names are side-by-side on the Vietnam Wall," I said. "Keith was awarded the Silver Star for trying to save a fellow Marine when he died. It appears TD was the Marine he was trying to save."

"And you say they both had closed coffins?" Mike asked.

"We only know about Keith," I said. "But the casualty notification officer who came to the house said he was killed by a large mortar blast, and that's why the coffin was sealed. I assume TD's body was just as mauled."

Mike sat back in his chair and yawned. "Okay, Pete, that's all. You going to write a story about this?"

"No," I said. "Even if I wanted to—which I don't—I'm too close to it."

"Good," Mike said.

I stood and stepped toward the door.

"And Pete?" Mike said. I turned back to him. "Remember, this is a police matter. Don't go sticking your nose into it like you usually do."

"I don't stick my nose into anything anymore, Mike. I get dragged in," I said. "I'm tired of murders."

"Me, too," Mike said.

I stepped through the door, paused, and turned around. "Oh, Mike?"

McCarty looked up from his desk. "Yeah?"

I held up my left hand with the pinky and index fingers extended. "Cowabunga, dude."

Jo called my cell as I was getting into the Mustang. She had come by the bungalow and found "poor little Jack starving," so she fed him a second dinner. He gobbled it up.

I waited until I got home to tell Jo about Rhonda and filled her in on what I learned from McCarty. When I finished, she sat in silence, thinking, then said, "Huh."

"Huh, what?" I asked.

"I never knew that about bodies not floating," she said. "You always see them float in the movies and TV."

"You were a landlubber army cop," I said. "I bet Navy cops know that."

"Not the ones I knew," she said. "So, what are you going to do now?"

"I told Mike I wouldn't interfere with Rhonda's murder investigation," I said.

"I would hope not," Jo said.

"I still want to find out what happened to Keith and TD," I added. "I drove up to the UCSD library today and found a published history of the Da Nang battle. Each Marine killed or wounded was mentioned, except for Keith and TD. Why? An accidental omission?"

"That's possible," Jo said.

"Or an overt omission?"

"That's possible, too. We both know that."

The government had tried to cover up the friendly fire incident that injured Jo and killed her MPs. We had joined forces and uncovered what really happened.

"So, I ask again," Jo said. "What are you going to do?"

I took out my reporter's notebook and flipped through the pages. "I took down the name of every Marine wounded, and then some others," I said. "I'm hoping I can track down someone who knew Keith and can tell me what happened."

"And how do you expect to do that?" Jo asked.

I shrugged. "I thought I'd start with local veteran associations," I said. "Maybe some of Keith's Marines stayed in the area. If not, I'll start branching out to other counties, even states. I know which outfit he was in. There could be a reunion group or something."

Jack sauntered into the living room, sat, and studied each of us as if making up his mind. Decision made, he trotted over to Jo and jumped onto her lap.

"Type up a copy of your list and email it to me at work," she said as she rubbed Jack's ears. "I still have some contacts at DoD, and some means of looking people up that you're not supposed to know about." She smiled sweetly at me.

I smiled back at her. "I knew I kept you around for some reason."

"I *know* why you keep *me* around," Jo said, her sweet smile turning lascivious. "And you know why *I* keep *you* around."

My smile grew wider, and I moved closer to her. She picked up Jack and held him up to me. "For our child," she said. "Now kiss little Jack goodnight."

I've heard that 3 a.m. is called the witching hour not because hags in black hats fly their brooms through the dark at that hour, but because it is the time of night at which most people wake with insomnia. I found little comfort in the thought that millions of insomniacs were lying awake, staring into the dark at the same time as I was. Jo lay beside me on her back, her breathing slow and soft. Jack curled on her stomach, snoring softly. And I was wide awake and thinking about Rhonda White.

Her death left me bereft, not because I would miss her in my life. I hadn't seen her for almost a quarter of a century. Yet, despite that absence, she represented a time in my life when I was still happy, a time when dreams were something I hoped would come with the future and not nightmarish memories of my past that haunted my sleep, a time when my parents and Keith were still alive, Rhonda was young and vivacious, and I was innocent. Rhonda was the last remnant of those long-ago years, and now she was gone, and I felt more alone than ever.

I threw back the covers and got up, slipped on a pair of jogging shorts and a T-shirt, and stopped short of reaching for my nightmare stash of cigarettes in the nightstand. If I lit up even outside, Jo would smell the tobacco smoke and wake. I didn't want that. Like me, Jo had her own ghosts, and I wouldn't deprive her of the rare chance for a sound sleep. As I watched her, Jack opened his eyes, lifted his head, and glared a warning at me, then went back to sleep.

Padding out of the bedroom, I quietly opened the front door and stepped out onto the porch. There was no marine layer, and despite the streetlights, I could see the stars flick-ering overhead. Lindbergh Field's flight hours hadn't begun yet, and the streets were quiet, allowing me to become lost in my thoughts and memories.

I was still there when the sun peeked over the foothills to the east three hours later.

"Petey, hurry up," Rhonda called as Keith loaded his surfboard into his used 1960s Mustang.

It was the summer between Keith's junior and senior years in high school, a year before he graduated and en-listed. I ran from the house, my arms, legs, face, and torso lathered with some sunscreen my mother insisted I wear.

"Come on, little brother, surf's up!" Keith yelled, as he settled into the driver's seat.

Keith was tall and thin, his light-brown hair long and bleached by the sun. He wore sporty wrap-around sun-glasses, surfer shorts, and a Hawaiian shirt left unbuttoned. His skin was sun-bronzed, and he looked like a god to me.

Rhonda—Keith insisted on calling her Rhonnie—sat in the passenger seat. Her dark hair was long and straight, her face youthfully cherubic and tanned. Over her two-piece bathing suit, she wore a coverup that left only her long, thin but shapely legs exposed. To me, she was a goddess.

At nine, I was short and squat, not having yet grown out of my baby fat. That wouldn't come for another couple of years. I wore swim trunks and a T-shirt I wouldn't take off when we got to the beach. I was embarrassed by my chubbiness. Yet, Keith—and more, Rhonda—always insisted I join them when they went surfing; it made me feel wanted, part of them. And I loved them for that.

"Everybody ready?" Keith asked.

"Let's go!" Rhonda said.

And as Keith accelerated the Mustang, I cried, "Cowabunga!"

Chapter 7

LOCATING MEMBERS OF KEITH'S old Marine Corps unit was more difficult than I expected. I spent two days looking up and calling veterans groups. I found a reunion group for his battalion, but, as the chairman of the group reminded me, a Marine battalion has six hundred or more troops. Also, Keith's battalion had seen service in Vietnam before he joined it—in fact, in one form or another, it also saw service in the Korean War and WWII. The number of veterans who served in that unit far exceeded the six hundred or so that guarded the airfield during the Easter Offensive of 1972. Nevertheless, I emailed my list of Marines to him with the hope he might match one or more of the names to his mailing list.

My luck with the local chapters of veterans groups was much the same. A few didn't keep updated records. Others told me to contact their national headquarters for any information about their members. After hours of dialing, talking, beseeching, and running up an outrageous telephone bill, I was as empty-handed as the day I was born.

Fortunately, Jo had better luck.

Through whatever connections or mojo she had, she produced the contact information for a half dozen names on my list who still lived in the county. The first two I called had never heard of Keith or TD. One didn't want to talk about the war. Another had passed away. Finally, one man on my list remembered Keith.

"Sure, I remember Sergeant Brandt," said Aaron Lemieux in a slow southern drawl. "He was in my platoon. A good Marine."

I explained that "Sergeant Brandt" was my brother, and I was trying to reconstruct the last days of his life for a family history I was writing. Yes, it was a lie, but sometimes a polite lie works better than the harsh truth.

"Well, I didn't see him killed," Lemieux said, pronouncing it *killt*. "But I can tell you what we was doing up before that." He paused, apparently thinking. "Hmmmm, you know, I got a buddy who was there, too—Scott Alexander. Maybe you want to talk to him, too?"

I looked at my list. Scott Alexander was the last name on it. "Sure," I said. "That'd be great."

After a few hours of phoning back and forth, Lemieux and Alexander agreed to meet me the next day for lunch at a VFW post in Poway. After the last call, I sat back in wonder at my luck. I'd found a needle in the proverbial haystack. In the back of my head, I thought I heard a someone say, "Good work, squirt."

It sounded like Keith's voice.

The next morning, I fed Jack, took a run, then took a shower. As I stepped out of the bathroom, the phone at my desk rang. It was Mike McCarty.

"Hey, what's up, Moondoggie?" I asked.

"You know I could have you arrested for harassing a police officer," he said.

"For calling you Moondoggie?"

"I could always claim that was some kind of veiled gangbanger threat," Mike retorted. "I'm a cop. Who are they going to believe? Me or some hack reporter?"

"Let's start over," I said. "What's up, Lieutenant McCarty, sir? How's that?"

"Better, but work on it," McCarty said. "I got the M.E.'s report. Your friend Rhonda White was definitely choked before entering the water. Her trachea was crushed."

"Just as you guessed," I replied.

"Yeah," Mike grunted. "We processed the shoes and purse we found and—maybe not too surprisingly—they were wiped clean of fingerprints."

"Meaning they were planted there by whoever choked Rhonda."

McCarty grunted again. "I followed up on some of the stuff you told me the other day about the victim."

"And?"

"I talked to her coworkers, the two guys she came out here with to meet with Danner," Mike explained. "They agree she didn't appear suicidal to them. Said she was distracted, something about being back in San Diego reminding her of an old boyfriend who was killed in Vietnam. I assume that's your brother."

"What about Danner?"

"Yeah, I went to his office—it's in an industrial park in Kearny Mesa," Mike said. "He remembered meeting Ms. White along with her coworkers, said she seemed a little off to him. She ran off to the restroom after she was introduced to him and when she came back, it looked like she'd been crying."

"Rhonda told me she ran to the restroom to compose herself after recognizing Danner as TD," I said.

"He said he never saw her again after that meeting," Mike added.

"And you believe him?"

"His mouth was twitching the entire time I was talking to him," McCarty said.

"So, you don't believe him?"

"I ran him through NCIC," Mike said, referring to the FBI's computerized National Crime Information Center. "Nada. In fact, I put him through every database I have access to, but it seems the man didn't exist until he showed up here in San Diego two years ago."

"Same results I came up with," I said. "Did you try running his fingerprints?"

"I'd need a warrant to get his fingerprints," Mike said, "and I don't have probable cause for a warrant."

"But you think he killed Rhonda," I said.

"I never said that. I was just following up on what you told me."

"If he is TD, and he's hiding from someone, that's motive to kill her, isn't it?" I asked. "To keep her quiet?"

"I checked this TD's service record, too," Mike said. "It said he died in Vietnam in 1972."

"Meaning?"

"Meaning we have nothing connecting Danner to your brother's friend," Mike said. "TD's dead."

"So is Rhonda," I said. "What about her?"

"I still have a murder to solve," McCarty said. "Just because I don't have a suspect at this time doesn't mean I'm going to drop the case. I have people out talking to hotel employees and collecting video from the security cameras around her hotel and nearby parking lots. It will take a few days to process what they get. Maybe we'll spot something."

"I hope so," I said.

"Just keep your nose out of it, Pete," Mike warned me again.

"I will, Mike," I said. "And Mike?"

"Yeah?"

"Thanks for the call, Moondoggie."

There was something like a growl at the other end, then the line went dead.

Chapter 8

POWAY IS A CREATURE of its own. It sits at the far eastern side of San Diego where the foothills grow into mountains. Once it was purely an agricultural community. But urban growth along the coast pushed more and more residents eastward, seeking a simpler, rustic locale to live in, even though they would have to commute twenty or more miles to work and back in rush-hour traffic. New homes built to house those seeking the country lifestyle led to urban sprawl that crowded out the old farms, ranches, and woodlands, leading to the community's nickname, "The City in the Country."

It's about twenty miles from my Ocean Beach bungalow to Poway as the proverbial crow flies. But crows have the luxury of flying over the traffic. They don't have to endure the congestion along Highway 52 to the east, the I-15 to the north, then east on Poway Road. In the morning, the tide of traffic from Poway and other communities in rural east county rolled down from the foothills, flooding the west- and south-bound lanes of the urban freeways. In the afternoon, the tide changes, flooding the north- and east-bound freeway lanes. Fortunately, I was heading east in the late morning after the rush hour began to ebb. Still, it took me the better part of an hour to push through traffic before I reached Poway.

The VFW post in Poway was a large trailer with aluminum siding, a fenced-in patio for outdoor dining shaded by a red, white, and blue awning sporting an American flag that fluttered overhead. Two black men sat at a table in the awning's shade, sipping on what looked like iced tea with lemon slices. I walked up and introduced myself.

Aaron Lemieux was a large man, well over six feet and nearly as wide, with a toothy grin to match. He wore a brown T-shirt and shorts. The left sleeve of his T-shirt was empty and as he stood to shake my hand, I noticed the lower part of his left leg was artificial. Scott Alexander was the complete opposite of Lemieux, shorter and gaunt, almost frail, with all four limbs intact. His jeans, black polo shirt, and jacket hung loose on him. We shook hands and sat down.

"Well, well, Sergeant Brandt's kid brother, eh?" Lemieux said, glancing me over. "A good man, Sergeant

Brandt. It's good you're trying to remember him—like with—what'd you call it? A family history? Nice to be remembered."

Alexander watched me with narrowed eyes. "You look awful young to be Keith's brother," he said.

Where Lemieux had a deep, resonant voice, Alexander's was a scratchy whisper. I realized he was not a well man.

"I was only ten when he died," I said.

"Whoa," Alexander said. "Your mama must've had a shitload of kids. You the youngest?"

I shook my head and gave him a bashful smile. "Just me and Keith," I said. "I was an accident. Dad's rubber broke."

Both men laughed, Lemieux with a deep belly hoot and Alexander with a cackle.

Lemieux slapped the tabletop with his one hand and said, "Canteen just opened. You hungry?" I nodded. "Good. Let's get some."

"I'm buying," I said.

"Damn right you are," both men said at the same time, and laughed.

Lemieux and I ordered burgers and iced tea. Alexander considered the menu and ordered soup and more tea. As we waited for our order, he seemed to study my face. "Don't you never take off those dark glasses?" he finally said. "Wonder how you can see in here."

"Sorry, forgot I was still wearing them," I said.

I took off the aviator sunglasses and hooked them on my shirt. As I did, Lemieux and Alexander grimaced at the scar running over and under my left eye.

"What happened to you?" croaked Alexander. "You lose a fight?"

"Sort of," I said. "A Salvadoran soldier butted me with his rifle."

"Salvadoran soldier?" said Lemieux. "What were you doing down there?"

"Covering the war," I explained. "I was a reporter with a news wire."

"Why'd he clobber you?" Alexander asked, his eyes narrowing again.

"He didn't want me to photograph what he and his friends were doing."

"Which was?" Alexander again.

"Bayonetting a mother and her baby."

"Shee-it," Alexander muttered and wiped his lips with his hand.

After that, we didn't say much until our orders came. Lemieux took a bite of his burger and chewed it as he studied me. With his mouth still full, he mumbled, "So, what was you? One of them war reporters?"

"War correspondent," I said, nodding. "I spent a few years down south in Central America covering the wars in

El Salvador and Nicaragua. The U.S. invasion of Panama. Then the Middle East for Desert Storm."

"Shee-it," Alexander said again. "You *volunteer* for that crap? You crazy or what?"

"My girlfriend says so," I replied. "She was in Desert Storm with the army."

Alexander shook his head. "Damn, what kind of damn foolish kids are we raising these days?"

He took a sip of his soup, and I turned the conversation back to Keith and their time in Vietnam.

"So, as I said on the phone, I was hoping you could help me piece together what happened the day Keith was killed."

They both looked at each other, then Alexander nodded at Lemieux. "You go," he said, his voice sounding even more hoarse.

"Well, to begin with, we was never supposed to be there," Lemieux began. "We was to stay offshore on the am-phibs as what they called a 'deterrence force' to keep Char-lie in line. The war was basically ending—for us, at least. Then Charlie attacked the south on Easter Day and the MAG got sent in to give the ARVN air support."

"MAG?" I asked.

"Marine Air Group," Alexander said, his voice now al-most a whisper.

"The MAG went in and, a little while later, Charlie hit them with rockets," Lemieux continued. "So, in May, our battalion flew in to provide security. Not that we could provide much of that against rockets. Most of us were green shits—you know, no combat experience, 'cept the senior officers and higher up NCOs.

"We set up a defensive perimeter, patrolled the bush outside the base—the usual stuff. At night, Charlie would throw more rockets at us. You know, after a while it became routine—"

"Routine!" cackled Alexander, shaking his head. "Routine! Sure, until that night they hit us hard."

"They hit us with rockets, mortars, and finally sappers," Lemieux continued. "The sappers made it through the perimeter wire—they was after the planes, you know. At that point, it was mostly close-in small arms fire, only it was so dark we didn't know who we were shooting at."

"That's when I got hit," Alexander said. "AK round in the gut. Took out a bunch of my intestines."

That's why he's so frail, I told myself.

"Grenade in my fighting hole got me," Lemieux said. "I heard it thump as it landed and leaped right out of that hole without thinking—instinct like, you know?" He nodded toward his empty shirt sleeve. "Not fast enough, though."

"That's terrible about your injuries," I said limply, not knowing how else to respond. "Both of you."

The big man shrugged. "I'm better off than some of the other guys, 'specially those who didn't make it," he said.

"With this peg leg, I can get around pretty good. And I still have one good hand to drink beer with." He laughed his barrel laugh.

"More like …" Alexander pumped his fist, simulating masturbation, and cackled.

"Can you tell me what happened to Keith?" I asked.

"We heard he was killed trying to save another Marine," Lemieux said. "Um, what was his name …?"

"TD," Alexander said with something like a sneer.

"Yeah, yeah, TD." Lemieux shook his head.

"You heard?"

"Like I told you on the phone, we didn't see him get it," Lemieux said. "Sometime later, our platoon lieutenant visited us in the hospital and told us what happened. TD got hit out in the open and your brother went after him. A mortar round—probably one of them big ones, like an 82mm—landed on top of them." He paused and shook his head. "Funny, I never knew they was on base that night."

Alexander stared into his soup and nodded.

"What do you mean?" I asked.

"Well, both of them wasn't supposed to be there on base that night," Lemieux said.

I stopped taking notes and looked at Lemieux. "What do you mean? Where were they supposed to be?"

"They was supposed to be in Saigon."

Chapter 9

"WHY SAIGON?" I ASKED.

"They was on a pass," Lemieux said. "Somehow they swung a forty-eight-hour pass and caught a chopper to Saigon."

"Well, Keith didn't swing it," Alexander said. "He didn't want it. I happened by the L-T's hootch and heard them arguing over it. Keith wanted to stay with the platoon, but the lieutenant ordered him to go to Saigon with TD."

The two men glanced at each other, then shook their heads. "TD," repeated Lemieux. "There's someone you'd like to forget."

That piqued my interest. "You didn't like him?"

"Wasn't nothing there to like," he said. "Fucking malingerer. Always had a scam going."

"Even on the ship—before we got sent in—he had scams going on," Alexander growled. Little prick never got pass PFC."

"Well, he did make lance corporal, but he lost it in an Article 15," corrected Lemieux.

"Article 15?" I asked.

"Nonjudicial punishment," Lemieux said. "Commanding officer's prerogative. What the Navy calls a 'captain's mast.' "

"Doesn't sound like someone my brother would have as a friend," I said.

"Keith was the only one in the platoon who put up with him," Lemieux said. He gave his head a long double shake. "Never understood why. We were all happy when TD left the platoon."

"He left the platoon?"

"Yeah, right after we landed at Da Nang," Alexander croaked. "As typical, he wrangled hisself a deal and got transferred to the battalion supply company. Cush job. No patrolling the bush. Like we told you, he was always scamming."

"But if TD wasn't in your platoon anymore, how did he and Keith get killed together?"

Alexander shrugged his thin shoulders. Lemieux frowned and shook his head.

"Don't know," he said. "Like I says, they was supposed to be in Saigon. They must've come back early before the attack started. After that, who knows what happened? When you're in a firefight, all you see is this tiny little slice of what's going on. You don't see the whole battle."

I nodded. "But your lieutenant said he saw Keith get killed?"

"The looey just *told* us what happened," Alexander answered. "Don't know if'n he actually *saw* it happen. Maybe one of the other grunts saw it and told him."

"I suppose you could ask him," Lemieux said.

"Your lieutenant?"

The big man nodded.

"How do I find him?" I asked. "What's his name?"

"Candee," Lemieux said. "Jason Candee. And you can find him at Camp Pendleton. That little shavetail is now a full bird colonel."

After writing the name in my notebook, I took the two photos Rhonda gave me from my pocket. I laid the brochure photo of Thomas Danner in front of them. "Do you recognize this guy?"

Lemieux and Alexander studied the photo, frowning and shaking their heads.

"Never seen him before," said the big man.

"Kinda looks familiar," Alexander said, "but I can't place him. Who is he?"

I placed the photo of Keith, Rhonda, and TD on the table.

"Lookie there!" Lemieux said. "It's your brother."

"And TD," added Alexander with distaste. "Who's the looker?"

"That's Rhonda," I said. "She was Keith's fiancée."

"Oh, yeah," Lemieux said, picking up the photo and studying it. "Yeah, I remember. I met her once, before we shipped out."

He laid the picture down, and I pointed to TD with one finger and to the portrait of Danner with another. "Now, does this guy Danner look familiar?"

They eyed both photos. Lemieux said, "Well, this Danner guy looks kinda like TD—"

"He's even got the same scraggly little mustache—"

"And the nose, too. Could be TD's brother."

"Did he have a brother?" I asked.

Lemieux shrugged his massive shoulders. Alexander said, "Never talked about his family. Don't think he had one."

"Who is this guy and what's it matter he looks like an older TD?" Lemieux knitted his brow as he glared at me.

My cover story blown, I fell back on the truth. "Rhonda called me a few days ago and said she met this guy Danner. She insisted he was TD, right down to a Marine Corps tattoo on his arm."

"But TD's dead," the big guy said. "Like your brother."

"That's what I told Rhonda," I said. "But a day or two later, she was dead. Murdered."

Both men recoiled from that. "How you know she was murdered?" demanded Alexander.

"The cops determined that," I replied.

"What now? You playing detective and trying to find her killer?" Alexander asked.

I shook my head. "I'm leaving that to the cops. I'm trying to find out what happened the day Keith and TD were killed. If they *both* were killed. If there is any chance in hell this Danner *is* TD, like Rhonda believed."

"I see," said Lemieux. "And if'n he was TD, you think that might be a good 'nough reason to kill Keith's girlfriend?"

I nodded.

Alexander suddenly grimaced and clutched his stomach. "Big L, I need to get home and take one of my pills."

"Are you okay?" I asked.

"We need to go," Lemieux said. He placed his big hand on Alexander's shoulder with more tenderness than I would expect from such a big man. "Scotty's not well."

Alexander was still gripping his abdomen. "Is it your wound acting up?" I asked.

The frail man slowly closed his eyes and shook his head. "I got the Big C," he said. "From Agent Orange."

I started to tell him I was sorry but stopped and just nodded. There was nothing to say to the victims of Agent Orange, the toxic defoliant the U.S. sprayed everywhere in Vietnam to deprive the Viet Cong of their jungle hiding places. It was supposed to save American lives and, perhaps, it did—for a while. But in the years following the war, over three hundred thousand American veterans died from various cancers caused by exposure to the agent, five times the number of Americans killed in action during the war. The number of Vietnamese who died due to exposure to the toxin was even higher.

We shook hands, and I watched the two veterans amble way, Lemieux limping on his artificial leg, his one hand gripping Alexander's left elbow to steady his ungainly gait. I wondered what Keith's life would have been like had he survived the war. He might have come home maimed like Lemieux. Or he might have died early from the effects of Agent Orange. Or he might've taken his own life with a gun or alcohol or drugs like so many war veterans do to escape the demons from their past. Or he might have married Rhonda and lived happily ever after.

I paid the bill and went home.

Chapter 10

THE NEXT MORNING, I fed Jack and took a run. When I returned, I found Jack sitting at the open bathroom door watching Jo shower. His head turned, and he glowered at me with big, dark eyes.

"What do you think you are, Jack?" I grumbled as I stepped over him. "A Peeping-Tom Cat?"

"That you, Peter?" Jo called from the shower. "Who are you talking to?"

"Jack, my Peeping-Tom Cat. He's been watching you shower."

"I know that," Jo said. "He's my lifeguard."

I kicked off my shoes and tugged off my running shorts and shirt, then stepped into the shower.

"No, I'm your lifeguard. He's a Peeping-Tom Cat," I said. "Now, can I give you some mouth-to-mouth?"

Jo giggled and Jack protested with a loud howl, but I kissed her anyway.

"Don't start something *we* can't finish," she said.

"Who says I'm starting something?"

"I can feel you starting down there."

"So?"

"I need to get to work …"

"So do I."

"You work here at home, Peter."

"No, I'm starting work right here."

"Well, I'm *going* to work," Jo said, slipping from my arms and stepping out of the shower. "I guess you'll have to finish your *work* by yourself."

As she dried off, Jack pranced around her ankles.

"Oh, by the way, your friend McCarty called," she said.

"What'd he say?"

"Just to call him back," she said. "I'm dressing now, Peter. I'm running late."

I turned off the hot water and let the shower run cold.

☼

"McCarty."

"Hey, Moondoggie," I said. "You called?"

Mike sighed. "Yeah, but for the life of me, I don't understand why I bother." After a pause, he added, "So, you're living with that army cop woman now?"

"Noooo," I said. "And she's not an army cop anymore. She's a security executive. And her name is Jo."

"She seems to be there every time I call you."

"She likes my cat," I said.

"Whatever," Mike replied, then changed the subject. "I thought you might be interested in what happened to me this morning."

"Go on."

"First thing as I walk into the station, I get a call from U.S. Customs."

"No doubt demanding to know what drugs or other contraband you smuggle into the country in your hollowed-out surfboards," I said. "I always thought those international surfing tournaments you go to were suspicious."

"Funny," Mike retorted. "They wanted to know why I was looking into a certain Mr. Thomas Danner."

I gripped the phone. "What?"

"You heard me."

"But how could they know?"

"My guess is when I ran his name through NCIC, it set off an alert," Mike said.

"What did they want to know?"

"A special agent asked why I was doing a background on Danner. I told them—truthfully—that he was a person of interest in a homicide. He asked how we linked him to the victim. And I told him a friend of the victim told me about Danner."

"And?"

"And then he asked me what the name of the friend was," Mike replied. "And I told him—again, truthfully—it was a nosy, prying, washed-up reporter named Peter Brandt."

"Oh, you're too kind," I said. "What did the special agent say?"

"Nothing. He just started laughing. When he finally stopped, he said—and I quote—'Tell the prick to call me.' Do you need his name?"

"No," I said. "I have a good idea who it is."

Dick Sanders was of average height, average looks, with average length dark hair flecked with gray. His face was rather boyish-looking and easily forgettable, and he spoke with a pronounced Brooklyn accent that was not. He reminded me of a mid-level CPA with some accounting firm that had a knack for embezzlement, which suited Sanders just fine because that's what he wanted people to believe. As an undercover agent with U.S. Customs, it was his job to infiltrate businesses illegally selling American technology or weapons to overseas buyers.

I met Sanders about the same time I met Jo, back when she and I were investigating the friendly fire incident that left her injured during Operation Desert Storm. Sanders was looking into a plot by American weapons contractors to secretly re-equip Iraq's army. Both our investigations led to the same culprits. Our paths crossed again a few months earlier when the murder of Jo's husband revealed a plot to resurrect the Nazi Party here in the United States.

Sanders wanted to meet at an open-air coffee bar in OB. The café had a Jimmy Buffett vibe with thatched fencing from which hung dozens of surfboards, the kind of place Mike McCarty would love. I had no difficulty spotting Sanders. Most of the clientele were twenty-something men sporting shorts, tank tops, and sandals, and twenty-something women in yoga tights or translucent beach tops covering thong bikinis. Sanders, on the other hand, was wearing a three-piece pinstriped suit and dark glasses. Gold bracelets glinted on both wrists, one below an expensive Rolex watch, all of which was "flash" for his corrupt businessman persona.

The older man sitting with Sanders was equally as incongruous. He wore a blue lightweight linen suit with a matching trilby hat, a white shirt topped by a bowtie. Horn-rimmed glasses perched on a prominent nose attached to a rectangular face with heavy jowls. He was the epitome of a university professor, which he once was before the Mossad, Israel's foreign intelligence service, recruited him. His name was Tygard, and he was a spy.

I sat down at their table without waiting for an invitation and leaned toward them. "You know, you two look very conspicuous considering you're supposed to be working undercover."

"Nonsense, Mr. Brandt," said Tygard. "Sometimes it's more inconspicuous to stand out in a crowd."

"That something from your spy manual?" I asked.

Tygard nodded. "I believe it's in chapter thirty-four." He smiled, amused by his wit.

"I'm hanging out at a beach coffee bar ogling all the girls in their teeny-weenie bikinis," Sanders said. "Just your typical fucking lecherous, corrupt businessman."

Sanders removed his dark glasses, leaned across the table, and asked, "How do you know Thomas Danner?"

"I don't know him," I said. "In fact, I've never met him."

"That's not what the cops say."

"What Lieutenant McCarty told you was that I mentioned his name in connection with a murdered woman," I told him. "It's the murdered woman I knew."

"How did you know the murder victim?" Sanders demanded.

I sighed. "That's a long story and if I'm going to tell it to you, I'm going to need some coffee." I stood and made my way into the pseudo-thatched hut and placed my order. As I waited for it, I collected my thoughts, deciding what to tell them and what not to tell them. Journalists, spies, and law enforcement officers all deal in information. Sometimes it's a good idea to hold some of that information in reserve.

When I returned, Sanders was still there but Tygard was not. I met Tygard for the same reason I met Jo and Sanders. Though I didn't like that he worked for the Mossad—an organization known for assassinations—I respected his abilities as an agent. That and he once saved my life.

"Where's Tygard?" I asked. "Or whatever his name is these days?"

"He'll be back," Sanders said. "Now, tell me about this woman you know."

I sat down and sipped my coffee. "Her name is—was—Rhonda White. She was an old friend of my family, and she was in town on business, so we got together for drinks at her hotel."

"How did she know Danner?"

"Her business in town was with him," I said. "She worked for some tech company, and he was interested in placing an order with them."

"For what?"

I shrugged. "We didn't talk about that."

"What did you two talk about?"

"Shouldn't you be doing this with a bright light in my face?" I asked. "Maybe a rubber hose?"

Sanders screwed his face up in annoyance. "Just answer the fucking question, Brandt."

"Just the stuff old friends talk about when they haven't seen each other in years," I replied. "How're the old folks—dead. Marriage and divorces—one for me, two for her. What a kick it was to be young once. That kind of stuff."

"That's all?" I nodded. "Then why did you tell the cops to look into Danner?"

"Moondog—I mean, Lieutenant McCarty—asked if she said anything that I thought was unusual. I remembered she mentioned this guy, Danner. Said she got a weird vibe from him, like they'd met before."

"Had they?" Sanders demanded.

"Had they what?"

Sanders screwed up his face again. "Had they met before?"

I shrugged again. I was trying to skate as close to the truth without being too truthful. "She said he kept looking at her strangely. I got the feeling it rattled her, even frightened her."

"That's it?"

I crossed my heart and held my right hand up in a three-finger Boy Scout salute. "Scout's honor," I said.

Chapter 11

WHETHER SANDERS AGREED, IT was my turn to ask questions.

"Now, you tell me why you're looking into Danner," I demanded.

"I'm the cop, Brandt," Sanders said. "I get to ask the questions."

"And I don't have to answer them," I replied. "I'm not under arrest. I haven't been read my rights. And I'm not under oath." Sanders protested, but I bulled on. "We've done this dance before, Sanders. You and I both know in a situation like this, information flows both ways. So, why do you find Danner interesting?"

Sanders leaned back in his chair, a smug smile on his lips. "I never said I did."

I responded with my own smug smile. "Okay, then I'll tell you why you *should* be interested in Danner. Customs handles stuff like stopping the illegal flow of dual-use technology out of the country, stuff that can be used for both commercial and military use. That's what *you* specialize in as a Customs undercover agent. Danner is some kind of technology consultant, only he doesn't know squat about tech. At least, that's what Rhonda told me. Rhonda said it was dual-use technology her company was negotiating to provide Danner. And since Tygard is with you, I suspect some of the technology is getting to countries not friendly to Israel. That's why you both *should* be looking into him. How am I doing?"

Sanders didn't respond. He faced me, but his sunglasses were so dark he could have been ogling some chick behind me. Finally, he said, "Is that all?"

"No," I said. "You should also be interested in him because Thomas Danner doesn't seem to have existed before he arrived in San Diego two years ago."

Tygard, the master spy, appeared next to the table and resumed his seat. He wasn't as dapper now. There was a small, dark stain on one sleeve of his coat and a small tear on one of his lapels. Both hands sported adhesive bandages, with another stuck to his cheek. He looked like he'd been mauled by a tiger. Which, it turned out, was pretty close to the truth.

"What the fuck happened to you?" demanded Sanders.

"You didn't tell me he had a pet mountain lion," Tygard said with distaste.

"You son-of-a-bitch," I growled. "You searched my house. If my cat—"

"Your … *cat*, if that's all he is … is fine, Mr. Brandt," Tygard said. "I can't say the same for myself, however."

"Well?" asked Sanders.

"Well, what?" Tygard said, scratching at the dark stain on his sleeve. "I never got past that wild creature …"

I leaned into Tygard. "Why did you try to search my place?" My words came out through gritted teeth.

"Call it due diligence, Mr. Brandt," Tygard said. "I— *we*—wanted to make sure it was okay to speak with you. It's been a while since last we met."

"It's only been a few months," I said. "For that, you broke into my house?"

"You can hardly call it breaking in," Tygard said. "I barely got through the front door when that saber-tooth tiger attacked me."

I made a mental note to make Jack a special dinner that night.

Tygard turned to Sanders. "Well?"

Sanders shrugged. "Sure, he's okay. Besides, he's pretty much guessed it all."

"I thought he would," Tygard said. He nodded to me. "I've always considered Mr. Brandt an intelligent and observant young man."

I leaned back. "And now it's your turn to share, Sanders."

Sanders shrugged, removed his dark glasses, and leaned forward.

"You guessed correctly, as far as you went," he said. "We believe he's a guy named Tobias Denton. Denton popped up on the CIA and Mossad radars in the Eighties because he was moving a lot of technology around Southeast Asia."

"You mean exporting tech out of Asia?" I asked.

"More import than export," Tygard said. "American technology into counties like Vietnam, Cambodia, and Laos that, at the time, were not U.S. trading partners. Some of that technology was also—shall we say 'forwarded'—to some of my country's not-so-friendly neighbors in Southwest Asia."

"Tobias Denton," I repeated, noting the familiar initials. "So, who is this guy? Where's he come from?"

Sanders shook his head. "We have no fucking idea. We believe he's an American, but he claimed he was Canadian and had a Canuck passport."

"Since Canada was not involved in the Southeast Asia wars of the 1960s and 1970s, being Canadian opened more doors for Mr. Denton," Tygard said.

"Yet, the Canucks have no fucking idea who Denton is—or was," Sanders said.

"Was?" I asked.

"Denton disappeared off our radar about three years ago," Sanders said. "Just about the time the U.S. began negotiating with Vietnam to become trading partners."

"We believe Mr. Denton realized that if the U.S. and Vietnam became trading partners, much of his business in illegal imports would dry up," Tygard said.

"So, he comes to the United States as Thomas Danner so he can become an exporter rather than an importer," I added.

"Exactly," Tygard said.

"And you have no idea where he came from before he showed up as Tobias Denton?"

"We think he was involved in small-time smuggling or black marketeering in the Seventies," Sanders said. "A lot of deserters in Vietnam ended up in the black market."

"The Seventies?" I asked. "You think this guy was a deserter?"

Again, the shrug. "Who the fuck knows? Why?"

I sat back and looked at the two operators, wondering if I should share more with them. That voice I'd been hearing in my head seemed to think I should. I reached into my pocket, took out the photos Rhonda had given me, and laid one on the table.

"This is the murdered woman," I said, pointing to Rhonda. "Rhonda was engaged to my brother, Keith." I pointed to Keith, then to TD. "This is Tommy Dykstra. He was Keith's friend in the Marines. People called him TD."

Tygard glanced at Sanders, but the agent merely said, "Okay. So?"

I placed the photo of Danner on the table, placed a finger on it and on the picture of TD. "Notice the resemblance?"

Both men studied the photos, then glanced at each other. Tygard nodded.

"This TD certainly looks like a younger image of Danner," he said.

"That's what Rhonda thought when she met him," I said. "In fact, she was *certain* it was him. While she and her business colleagues waited in the lobby of his office, she spotted Danner come out of the men's room without his coat and his shirt sleeves rolled up, like he'd just washed his hands. She saw he had a Marine Corps globe-and-anchor tattoo on his lower right arm, the same place Keith and TD had the globe-and-anchor tattooed on their arms. She also said TD had a nervous twitch at the corner of his mouth, and she saw the same twitch on Danner's mouth."

"So, where is this guy, TD, today?" Sanders asked.

"Dead," I said. "At least he's supposed to be dead. He and my brother were reported killed in the same battle in Vietnam in 1972, but …"

"But what?" demanded Sanders.

"My brother's funeral had a closed coffin," I said. "They got hit by some kind of large mortar shell and—well …"

"There wasn't much to identify or bury," concluded Tygard, nodding sadly. "I have seen it too many times with terrorist bombings in Israel."

"So, you never saw your brother's body," Sanders said. "And we can assume this TD's family never saw his. And, so, you're thinking—"

"*Rhonda* was thinking maybe TD wasn't killed in Vietnam as reported, and that Thomas Danner was, in fact, TD," I said. "I wasn't convinced, but I humored her and said I would take a look." I shook my head. "At the time, I thought she was grasping at straws, especially because she was certain that if TD was still alive, then my brother was, too. I think she believed if Keith were still alive, maybe they could get back together."

"You said, 'at the time' you thought she was grasping at straws," Sanders said. "What about now?"

"Then Rhonda got murdered," I said. "And the killer tried to make it look like suicide."

Tygard nodded. "And you began thinking maybe her murder was linked to Danner, perhaps because he is this TD and recognized her."

"It did cross my mind," I said. "Later, I managed to find a couple of guys who served with Keith. They fought in the battle at the Da Nang airfield where Keith and TD died, but they don't remember seeing them on base the night of the attack. In fact, they were surprised to hear they'd been in the battle."

"Why?" asked Sanders.

"Because they weren't supposed to be at Da Nang," I said. "They were supposed to be on R&R in Saigon."

Sanders and Tygard both sat back and thought about what I told them. Sanders frowned before speaking.

"You're not poking your nose into this Rhonda woman's murder, are you, Brandt?"

"I told Lieutenant McCarty I wouldn't," I said, "and I'm not."

"But you are—as Agent Sanders so quaintly put it—poking your nose into Thomas Danner's background," Tygard said.

"I'm just trying to figure out what really happened to my brother the night he supposedly died," I said.

"Sometimes it's better to let sleeping dogs lie," the Mossad agent said.

"I seem to remember telling Rhonda that," I said.

"You may not like what you discover," Tygard said.

"Why's that?"

"Because if Danner is your brother's friend, TD, and if TD is a deserter, then Miss White might have been correct in believing your brother is still alive," he said. "And if he is alive, then he would also be a deserter."

Chapter 12

THE NIGHT SKY WAS unusually clear. The marine layer that normally rolled in at night stayed away and San Diego Bay sprawled before the big window in Jo's new apartment like a thousand tiny, shimmering lights. A cruise ship steamed down the main channel beneath us, lit up like a sea-going Las Vegas standing out to sea. Far in the distance, on the other side of the border, we could see the flashing strobe of Tijuana's bull-fighting ring where some wretched animal was being tortured to death as we admired the view.

"When you said you got an apartment where you used to live, I didn't realize you meant the *same* apartment," I said.

"I contacted the landlord some months ago and told him if this apartment ever became available, I wanted it," Jo said. "A young Navy officer and her husband were living here, but she recently got new orders, so here we are."

Where we were was on the bay side of Point Loma, not far from the Navy's submarine base. Portuguese fishermen originally settled the area along with Italian immigrants. They founded the fishing industry that had once been one of San Diego's chief trades, providing the city's nickname "Tuna Capital of the World." In the Eighties, the tuna boats sailed off to foreign harbors where there were no seamen's unions and fewer regulations regarding the capture of dolphins in their nets. The canneries followed. Even the colorful, lateen-rigged fishing schooners moored Mediterranean style at the downtown quay disappeared. Now, gentrification replaced many of Point Loma's Portuguese families.

A clattering of claws on the hardwood floor interrupted our ruminating. Jack scurried down the hall, then threw himself on his side and slid across the bare floor until he bounced into the back of the sofa we were sitting on. He scrambled to his feet, ran back up the hallway, and repeated the maneuver.

"Looks like Jack is enjoying himself," Jo said.

Jo insisted I bring Jack. She had prepared a litter box in the bathroom and placed two bowls on her kitchen floor for water and kibble. She even bought Jack a cat bed to curl up in. But Jack was having too much fun body surfing on the hardwood floors to eat or nap.

"You're spoiling him," I said.

"Like you don't?"

"I think you're trying to lure him to stay here," I said. "His own bed, box, and food."

"Not just him," Jo said. "Come." She led me through the hallway to the bathroom. I noticed Jack had already used the box. Jo pointed to a bathroom cabinet holding a toothbrush, razor, and deodorant. "Those are yours."

I examined the razor. "It's a feminine razor," I said.

"It's all I had," Jo said. "Besides, you don't need more scars on your face."

I said "Humph," and turned to leave. We trailed Jack as he made another cannonball run down the hallway and resumed our places on the sofa.

"What's the matter, Peter?" Jo asked. "You've been somewhere else all evening."

I poured some more wine and took a long sip—more like a swig—before telling her.

"Remember Sanders and Tygard?"

"Of course."

"I met with them today."

Jo's eyebrows lifted as she sipped her wine. "Really? What for?"

"They're interested in Thomas Danner, too," I explained. "They think he's someone who used to operate in Southeast Asia named Tobias Denton. A technology smuggler. He brought dual-use stuff into the region to sell to countries where it wasn't supposed to go."

"That's why Sanders is interested," Jo said. "I see that. But why Tygard?"

"Some of the stuff went to Israel's neighbors," I said.

"I see that, too, now."

"Anyway, Tobias Denton disappeared about three years ago, just before Thomas Danner showed up here."

"Okay," Jo said.

"Denton claimed to be Canadian, but Sanders and Tygard think he was American," I explained. "Maybe someone who deserted during the Vietnam War and went into the black market. Apparently, a lot of deserters ended up in the black market."

Jo frowned. "Were there a lot of desertions during that war?"

Like me, Jo also lost a brother in Vietnam and, being a former army officer and daughter of an army general, the idea of deserters did not sit well with her.

I nodded. "I looked it up this afternoon. More than half a million."

Jo's wine glass stopped midway to her lips and her eyes widened. "Half a million?"

I nodded again. "But most of those took place outside of Vietnam; guys who walked away from their posts or ships in the States or in other countries. Only a few thousand deserted while in the combat zone."

"Still …" Jo shook her head.

"Tygard and Sanders believe this Tobias Denton deserted in the early 1970s, since he didn't show up until the latter part of the decade."

"And you're thinking this Denton/Danner is your brother's friend, TD," Jo concluded. I nodded. "Well, the initials are all the same. But it'd be pretty stupid to use names with identical initials if you were trying to hide your true identity."

"From what Rhonda and Keith's Marine Corps buddies told me, TD wasn't that bright, just a slacker and grifter," I said.

"Okay, let's assume Denton/Danner is TD," Jo said. "What about that has you upset? As I said earlier, you've been somewhere else all night."

"First, it gives Danner a damn good reason to kill Rhonda," I said.

"And second?"

"And second …" I hesitated, collecting my thoughts. "When I told them I was trying to find out what happened the night Keith was killed, Tygard warned me I might not like what I discovered."

"Why would he say that?"

"He said if TD deserted and is now Danner, then there's a possibility that Keith deserted with him."

Jo put down her glass and shook her head vigorously. "No, no, no," she said. "They don't give Silver Stars to deserters, Peter. You know that."

"I do," I said. "But if TD is alive, then what happened to Keith? Who was he trying to save when he got killed?"

"Maybe it was someone else," Jo said. "And maybe the bodies were so mangled they only *thought* one of them was TD's. When my MPs were killed, their bodies were so badly torn apart and burned, they had to be identified by DNA."

Jo's hand flew to her mouth as she tried to stifle a sob.

I slipped closer and put my arm around her. "Maybe," I said. Jo buried her face in my shoulder. "In fact, I'm sure you're right. Let's not talk about this anymore."

As Jo quietly sobbed, I stared out the window at the flickering lights on the bay, looking like mirror images of the stars hovering above them. But a moment later they seemed to morph turning into flashes of gunfire in the night. A thousand tiny guns spitting out death. Perhaps like the last thing Keith saw before …

The clatter of Jack's claws scampering along the hallway tore me away from my self-indulgent thinking, and I couldn't help but smile as he once again thumped into the back of the sofa.

Chapter 13

OVER THE FOLLOWING TWO days, I made little progress in discovering what happened to Keith and TD. Jason Candee, Keith's former platoon leader, was easy enough to find. Camp Pendleton prominently displayed his name, photo, and biography on its website. No longer the shavetail lieutenant that Keith, Alexander, and Lemieux served under, Candee was now a full colonel commanding an infantry regiment. His photograph showed a middle-aged officer with a long, thin face ending in a square jaw. He wore his gray-flecked hair cut short, but not shorn in the high-and-tight style worn by many Marines; more of a butch haircut like my father wore in the Fifties and Sixties. His bio read like a history of the United States' wars of the latter 20th century—Vietnam, Beirut, Panama, Grenada, and Operation Desert Storm.

Finding him and talking to him, however, were two different things. I spent three days trying to call him, winding my way through the Marine base's labyrinthine phone system. First, I called the base public information office, identifying myself as a writer working on a family history and wanted to talk with people who served with my brother. The PIO provided me with the phone number for Candee's division headquarters. Division headquarters gave me the number for his regimental offices. The regimental offices gave me the number for his headquarters staff. It was late afternoon by the time I got through to Candee's office, and the female Marine I spoke to told me the good colonel had left for the day.

The next morning, I called Candee's office again. Yes, the same Marine said, the colonel got my message, but was in meetings all morning and would return my call as soon as he could. I spent most of the day working on my next book and waiting for the colonel's call. By mid-afternoon, I grew tired of waiting and called again. A different Marine, a gruff gunnery sergeant, said Candee was still out of the office. Frustrated, I called Jo and whined about Candee avoiding me. An hour later, Jo called back and, having used her remaining contacts in the military, gave me Candee's personal military email address.

God, I love that woman.

I wrote Candee an email that I hoped would tug at his heartstrings, assuming someone who served in five wars still had heartstrings, or even a heart.

Colonel Candee,

My name is Peter Brandt. I am the younger brother of Sergeant Keith Brandt who served in your platoon in 1972 in Da Nang. I am writing a family history and have been talking to former members of your platoon to find more details about Keith's service in the Marines as well as his death at Da Nang airfield. If possible, I would like to speak with you as you were his platoon leader.

This meeting would mean a great deal to me. As I said, I am Keith's younger brother—his much younger brother (by ten years) and his only sibling. Like many younger brothers, I idolized Keith. Our parents have since passed, and I would very much like to memorialize them and Keith with this family history.

I thank you in advance for your time and consideration.
Peter Brandt.

There was little more I do but wait. I worked on the book with occasional breaks to check my email. There was nothing until that evening. Jo and I had gone out to dinner. She had an early-morning meeting, so I dropped her off at her apartment and went home. Jack greeted me at the door, mewing and wrapping himself around my legs before leading me into the kitchen to show me his kibble bowl was close to empty. I refilled the bowl and poured myself a scotch before sitting at the computer to read my email. There were inquiries from the newsweekly I reported for, not-so-gentle reminders of my impending book deadline from my publisher, and staff notices and announcements from the college where I taught journalism part-time.

Jack, licking kibble crumbs from his lips, jumped onto my lap and kneaded my thigh before curling up and making himself comfortable. As I sipped my drink and scratched Jack's head, a new email popped up. It came from an unfamiliar private email account. Being wary of computer viruses, I seldom opened emails from unknown senders, but something told me to open this one. It had only six words.

Mt. Soledad monument. 0800 tomorrow. Candee.

Mount Soledad looms over the wealthy San Diego enclave of La Jolla, its steep oceanside escarpment cluttered with gravity-defying mansions and faux French villas. Bordering its eastern escarpment is the I-5 freeway, which connects to a cut through the mountain's northern slope, providing the main access road to the seaside village. Atop its highest peak stands a three-story white cross, a war memorial which has for decades sparked dozens of legal battles between believers and nonbelievers. It's said the view from the monument, with the expanse of the Pacific to the west, and the rest of San Diego to the east, is one of the most beautiful in California, particularly at sunset.

It wasn't the first time a source wanted to meet at the monument. Except for Memorial Day and Veterans Day, the monument was rarely crowded. Joggers and bicyclists come to take a turn around the cross, tourists come to gawk at the sights, and day hikers explore the steep trails. It's easy to find a secluded spot for a confidential talk, and the prevalent ocean breeze whisks away the spoken word.

So, I was curious, to say the least, why Colonel Candee wanted to meet in such a place.

Jo said military custom was to arrive fifteen minutes early, whether you're attending a meeting or relieving a guard post. That meant Candee would arrive at the monument at 7:45 in the morning. I made sure I was there by 7:30. I always preferred having a source come to me, rather than me to him. Experience taught me it was safer that way.

Parking in the lower lot, I walked up to the monument and around its entire perimeter to make sure there were no surprises waiting for me. Climbing up to the cross itself gave me a three-hundred-and-sixty-degree view of the mountaintop.

Candee arrived at 7:46. I spotted his car, a sedate compact sedan, coming up the drive, a military vehicle sticker stuck to the lower left windshield. He parked, and I watched him unlimber himself from the vehicle. Candee was much taller than I expected, and trimmer than I thought a middle-aged man would be. He wore civvies, khaki slacks, and a blue polo shirt. He glanced around the base of the monument before looking at his wristwatch.

"Colonel Candee," I called.

He turned and looked at me but didn't move, making me climb down from the cross and come to him. So much for *my* preferences.

"Colonel, I'm Peter Brandt," I said, reaching him and holding out my hand.

"I know who you are, Mr. Brandt," he said without taking my hand. "You are a reporter and book author. I have one of your books, the one about Desert Storm."

I didn't ask if he enjoyed the book. Every reader considers themself a book critic.

"It wasn't bad," he said. "I liked the way you concentrated on the grunts, not the politicians and brass. Walk with me."

I followed along as he passed the rows of photographs of local men and women who served in the armed forces. We walked in silence for a while, stopping now and then to inspect a particular face. When he spoke, he didn't stop inspecting.

"I've been in five wars," he said. "I've commanded more Marines in combat than I can remember. It doesn't matter which war, the faces are always the same. The same is true here, with these faces. Sometimes when I look at photographs from wars before I was born, the faces are still all familiar to me."

He stopped so abruptly, I almost bumped into him.

"Do you know why that is?" he asked.

"Because they are all young," I said. "Young, in the prime of their lives. Innocent even."

Candee looked at me for the first time, his eyebrows raised. His mouth turned down, and he nodded. "Exactly." He thought about that a moment before saying, "And when we use them up in our wars, they are no longer young."

"And no longer innocent," I added.

"And no longer innocent," he repeated, nodding, and started walking again. "Let me be frank, Mr. Brandt. I do not believe you are writing a—what did you tell my staff? A family history. That's not the kind of stuff you write. So why are you interested in what happened to your brother—*if* he is your brother?"

I pulled the photo of Keith, Rhonda, and TD from my pocket and handed it to him. He studied it for a moment, a bleak smile coming to his lips. "Well, that's Keith Brandt all right," he said sadly. He looked up at me, then back to the photo. "And I do see a family resemblance." His sad smile turned to a grimace. "And that's his friend, TD." He handed the photo back to me. "I don't know who the girl is."

"Her name is—was—Rhonda White," I said. "She was Keith's fiancée. She was recently murdered here in San Diego. And it's possible her murder is somehow connected to Keith or TD."

Candee stopped again and scowled at me. "How can that be? They've been dead for over twenty years."

I handed him the photo of Thomas Danner. "Shortly before Rhonda died, she met this man. His name is Danner, Thomas Danner. But Rhonda swore to me he was Tommy Dykstra—TD."

Candee squinted at the photo, removed a pair of reading glasses from a pocket, put them on, and studied it again. "Let me see that other picture again." Holding both up to the morning light, he looked from one to the other. "There is a resemblance. But that's all I can say."

"Rhonda saw a globe-and-anchor tattoo on his right forearm, just like Keith and TD both had," I explained. "And Danner has the same facial tic as TD when he got nervous."

The colonel waggled his head left and right as he studied the photographs, hesitant to make a conclusion.

I continued. "A source in U.S. Customs said they believe Thomas Danner is actually a man named Tobias Denton who illegally imported technology into Southeast Asia.

Denton disappeared not long before Danner arrived in San Diego. They also know Denton wasn't his real name. They believe he was probably an American deserter who got involved with the black market in the 1970s." Candee pivoted toward me at the word *deserter*. "There is a possibility Danner and Denton and TD are all the same person, and that Rhonda was killed because she recognized Danner as TD."

Candee handed the picture back, shaking his head. "Can't be," he said.

"Why not?" I demanded. "Did you see their bodies? Keith's and TD's? Because we didn't. Keith's coffin was closed, and I believe so was TD's. For all my family and I know, their coffins could have been empty. So, did you see their bodies, colonel?"

He stood quietly for a long time, staring out at the ocean. Blinking twice, he turned to look back at the photographs surrounding the monument. He sighed and shook his head.

"Why not?"

He faced me, his eyes angry. "Because they weren't killed at Da Nang," he said. "They died in Saigon."

Chapter 14

CANDEE LOOKED AROUND, THEN gestured with his head toward a cement picnic table perched near the peak's edge. We sat on opposite sides, the colonel with his back to the table, staring out at the sea again as if seeing something far across the ocean, perhaps as far as Da Nang airbase.

"I want you to understand something, Brandt," he began. "I'm on my sunset tour."

"Sir?"

"Pendleton is my last posting before I retire," he explained. "I don't want anything to fuck up my retirement. Do you understand?"

"Yes, sir," I said.

"Do you?"

"You don't want anyone to know where I got the information you're about to tell me," I said.

He gave me a side glance and nodded.

"You want me to guarantee what you tell me will be confidential and off-the-record," I said.

"However you describe it in your journalistic jargon," he said, still staring at the ocean. "You and I never met. As far as we're both concerned, I never returned your phone calls."

"You have my word, colonel," I told him.

He turned and looked at me directly, his eyes burrowing into mine.

"If you're as good a man as your brother was, I believe you," he said.

I noted he said "was" in reference to Keith. So Candee *did* believe my brother was dead.

"What happened at Da Nang has stuck in my craw all these years," Candee went on. "I considered resigning my commission, I was so disgusted. But I was a young, inexperienced shavetail, and I went ahead and followed my orders."

"Which were?"

"I got called into my battalion commander's hootch," Candee explained. He bit his lower lip as he thought about how to continue.

"First, a little background. Your brother's friend, TD— God, I can't imagine why your brother put up with him. They were polar opposites. Your brother was a damn fine

Marine, a good leader, competent. TD was … well, TD. A malingerer. A grifter. Always looking out for himself. Always bragging about something or other."

Candee stopped and shrugged.

"Keith was a good older brother," I said. "Always looked out after me, no matter what kind of trouble I got in. Maybe he saw TD as another little brother."

A memory floated to the surface of my consciousness.

Chuckie Sims was a bully. He was big, fat, and dumb, and he liked to throw his weight around, usually in the form of his fists. He'd been my tormentor for a long time, and we'd been in more than a couple of scuffles. But he never fought anyone unless he had his rat pack of fellow toughs with him. At the first sign a fight wasn't going his way, they moved in. Chuckie didn't like me because no matter how many times they beat me, I never feared him.

We were in a big empty field that I took as a shortcut from school to my house. Chuckie had been antagonizing me all day, and I knew I'd have to fight my way through, probably to my detriment. His friends lined up on the little trail I used as my shortcut and began jeering and tossing little stones toward me as I passed. Chuckie stood in the middle of the trail like some fat southern sheriff at a roadblock.

"Hey, Brandt, where you think you're going?" Chuckie demanded.

"Home," I said, and brushed past him.

He stepped back in front of me. "Not this way you're not," he said. "This is my field."

"Who says?" Witticisms weren't my strong suit back then.

"I do."

I sighed and set my books on the ground. "Oh, yeah?"

"Yeah."

I sensed the others closing around us, forming a semicircle behind me like a wall to rein me in, and I took my stance.

Chuckie and I circled each other, tossing two or three feints, while the others hurled insults at me. Then I heard Keith's voice behind me.

"God damn you, Sims." Keith broke through the wall of toughs, pushing them aside like a ship's prow through the ocean.

"Oh, lookie," Chuckie said, "big, bad brother coming to protect little Petey ..."

"Keith, I don't need you—"

"Shut up, Pete," Keith said. He reached down with one hand, grabbed Chuckie by the shirt collar, and hauled him to his tiptoes. "I've fought your brother too many times not to know how you fight, you little fuck. You want to fight Pete, you do it yourself." He dropped Chuckie and turned to the

others. "Any of you try to interfere, you'll have to deal with me. You idiots understand?"

Heads bobbed, and slowly, one by one, Chuckie's backup crew slipped away, leaving only Chuckie, me, and Keith. I retook my stance in front of Chuckie, but I could see the fight—or was it his courage?—had left. He hocked a loogie on the ground and hitched up his pants.

"Ah, who cares about you anyway, you little turd?" he said, then turned away, following his pack.

When I came back to the present, the colonel was looking at me with dull blue eyes, absorbing what I said. He pursed his lips and nodded.

"Maybe," he said. "Could be. Anyway, not long after we landed at Da Nang, TD wangled himself a transfer to the supply company. Personally, I was happy to get rid of him. After that, we didn't see much of him. There was scuttlebutt he was taking a lot of chopper flights off base. Don't know where or why, but something to do with supply issues.

"So, back in my CO's hootch, the major tells me I needed to give your brother a forty-eight-hour pass. We'd only landed a few weeks before this and none of us needed R&R. The old man said he *had* to give TD a pass, and he wanted your brother to tag along with him to keep him out of trouble. I thought that was a chickenshit excuse, and so did your brother when I told him."

"One of your former Marines, Scott Alexander, told me he was passing by your … *hootch* … and overheard you two arguing about it," I told him.

Candee looked away and scratched his chin as he dug through old memories. I watched a smile come to his face. "Old Scotty," he said. "I remember him. How is he doing these days?"

"Dying of cancer," I said. "Agent Orange."

Candee winced, then let out a sigh. "Shit."

"Colonel," I prodded. "If we could continue. What happened in Saigon?"

He nodded. "Of course. But first you need to understand there was a big firefight the next night after the two of them took a chopper to Saigon. Charlie hit us with missiles, arty, stormed and breached the wire. At points, the fighting was hand-to-hand. We took a lot of wounded and some KIA before we forced them back. The next morning, we were licking our wounds—treating the wounded, sending out the dead, repairing our fortifications. The battalion CO calls me back to his hootch. This time there was a man in green fatigues, flak vest, steel pot, and carrying an M16, but he wasn't military. The CO introduced him as the Saigon station chief for NIS—Naval Investigative Service. Today, it's the Naval Criminal Investigative Service, or NCIS. That's when they told me Keith and TD were dead.

"The NIS agent explained TD had been involved in a large black-market ring, and he was going to provide NIS with information to take the ring down. TD was supposed to meet two of his agents in a Saigon bar and give them the information. Keith was sent along because NIS was afraid if TD went alone, it would look too obvious he wasn't on R&R. Guys never went on R&R alone, or so the NIS guy said.

"Keith and TD went to a bar where TD was to meet the NIS agents—though Keith didn't know that. Well, what I was told was that Keith left the bar just moments before a bomb went off. Your brother rushed back into the bar to help TD, and another bomb went off. Keith was killed, as well as TD and the two agents. The bombs started a fire and by the time the fire was out, the bodies were burned beyond recognition. Keith and TD were identified by their dog tags."

It was my turn to stare out to sea. My thoughts were a jumble. Images of Keith as we grew up, of him in his uniform, of him and Rhonda, of Mom and Dad so proud and yet worried for their eldest son. Everything Candee described played out in vivid scenes in my mind—the dank bar, the first blast, Keith running into the bar as the second blast came. The fire.

My heart pounded and my chest ached. My head spun like a top and I realized I wasn't breathing. Candee watched me and asked, "Are you okay, Brandt?"

I let go of the breath I was holding and nodded. I tried to say something, but the words wouldn't form. My mouth just opened and closed like the mouth of a landed fish.

Nodding, I forced a cough, then cleared my throat. "Sorry, colonel, it was just—"

"I understand," Candee said. "It's hard to hear how a loved one died. My oldest boy was killed in Desert Storm."

"Colonel, if Keith and TD were killed in Saigon by a bomb, why the charade about them being killed at Da Nang?"

Candee grimaced. "That was the cover up," he said. "The part I considered resigning over. The whole NIS thing was a SNAFU. You know what SNAFU stands for?"

"Situation normal—all fucked up," I answered.

Candee nodded. "NIS needed to cover its ass," he said. "Actually, I think the station chief needed to cover *his* ass. His little investigation got two of his agents and two Marines killed, and for what?"

"I don't understand," I said. "Why didn't NIS just take TD into their offices to have him give them the information they wanted?"

Candee glanced at me with a sardonic smile. "Exactly," he said. "That's what I asked. Why the theatrics of meeting in a bar? Especially in the middle of an enemy offensive? It made little sense, and I told them so." The colonel sighed, shaking his head again. "The battalion commander ordered me to stand down—that means to shut up. He said the NIS investigation was still ongoing and was too important for a shavetail lieutenant to understand. Then he ordered me to tell my men that your brother and TD were KIA—killed in action—*and* to put it in my after-action report. All the time, that damn NIS agent stood behind the CO with a smug smile on his face.

"You know, they say you see red when you're angry. That's how I felt. But the major was right. What did a junior officer know about the big picture? So, I snapped a salute, did an about-face, and marched the hell out of there. When I got back to my hootch, I wrote up my after action, describing Keith's and TD's deaths as close to the truth as I could. Then I wrote your brother up for the Silver Star. The old man wasn't happy about that, but he couldn't deny it."

Candee paused and thought about what he said. "Look, Brandt, don't get me wrong. I didn't recommend your brother for the Silver Star as just an angry gesture. He deserved it for running back into that bar to save TD. Sergeant Keith Brandt was a fine Marine, a good combat leader, and he deserved to be remembered as that, not the victim of some bureaucratic blunder."

He fell silent, and we both stared out at the ocean, the rising sun glinting off the undulating rows of whitecaps. A car came up the road and parked nearby. A man and woman got out, along with three kids—a family of tourists. The children dashed around the monument while their parents admired the view and took photographs. No one looked at the photographs of those who served.

"Thank you, Colonel Candee," I finally said. "For what you did for Keith and for telling me the truth. Do you happen to remember the name of the NIS station chief?"

Candee dug through his memories but shook his head. "I'm sure the CO told me, but I don't remember. Sorry. Why?"

"I'd like to talk to him," I said. "About the cover up—and TD."

Candee squinted at me. "You still think this guy—what's his name? Danner. You still think he could be TD?"

I shrugged. "I believe everything you told me—everything that you told me *you* were told. But there're still a lot of loose strings. Why does this man Danner look and act so much like TD, for one? And why was Rhonda murdered shortly after meeting him, for another? And why have his agents meet TD in a bar instead of their offices?"

The colonel studied me for a while, and a sad smile came to his face. "You really are your brother's brother," he said.

"I'll take that as a compliment, sir."

"You should." He stood and held out his hand. "Well, good luck, Mr. Brandt."

I shook his hand. "Peter," I said.

"Peter," he repeated with a nod.

I watched him walk back to his car and drive away, then walked down to the lower parking lot. As I reached my car, I saw a small green sedan pull away. The driver wore heavy glasses and a blue trilby hat.

Tygard, the Mossad agent.

Chapter 15

WHEN I GOT BACK to my bungalow, I made three phone calls.

The first went to Fred Danbury. Fred owned a travel office in Orange County, but a few lifetimes before he was a pilot for the CIA, flying covert missions throughout Southeast Asia and Africa for Air America, the agency's proprietary "airline." After retiring from "the Company," Fred settled down in Southern California. "Settled down," however, isn't the correct phrase for Fred Danbury.

I met Fred while covering Ronald Reagan's proxy wars in Central America. Fred was part of a group of volunteer anti-Red Americans providing equipment and training to the Contra rebels fighting Nicaragua's communist regime. He specialized in arranging the purchase and delivery of aircraft, and training Contra pilots how to use them to airdrop supplies to rebel units fighting in the jungle. Somehow, we bonded over drinks in some hotel bar and stayed in touch ever since. Which was good for me, because Fred also stayed in touch with his friends from the shadow world of espionage.

"Why, Peter Brandt!" Fred's laconic drawl drew out my name, making it sound like four syllables instead of three. "Boy howdy, how you doing? Been too many moons since we shared a bottle of rot-gut bourbon."

"Actually, Fred, I saw you only a few months ago," I reminded him. "We had a long talk about Nazi gold over a Mexican breakfast."

"Yeah, but we didn't drink no whiskey, boy." Fred snorted and I heard the click of a Zippo lighter, probably lighting one of the thin, black cigars he always smoked. I could envision him leaning back in his office chair, his shit-kicker cowboy boots perched on his desk, puffing on his cigarillo, the gray smoke curling around his hard, angular face with its neatly trimmed, sharply-angled moustache and his thinning shock of hair, both now sporting more gray than black. "So, what kind of mess do you want ol' Freddy to get you out of this time?"

"Just some information, Fred," I said. "I need the name of a guy who was the agent in charge of the Saigon station for the Naval Criminal Investigative Service station back in

1972. Back then it was the called the Naval Investigative Service—NIS."

I paused as Fred scribbled notes. "And just what would this here be regarding?"

"My brother died in a bomb blast in Saigon that year," I explained. "He was a Marine and somehow NIS was involved. I'm trying to find out how."

A memory suddenly flashed through my mind—the last time any of us saw Keith alive.

We were all dockside as Keith's battalion loaded onto the amphibious landing ship at the naval base in San Diego. We had only a few minutes with Keith until he had to fall in and shuffle aboard the ship, burdened with a sea bag, backpack, and M16 rifle. His long, sun-bleached hair was gone, replaced with a brown stubble. His face was still tan, and he somehow looked older.

He introduced us to some of his buddies. Mom and Dad and I hugged him goodbye. Rhonda hugged him last and longest. We watched him board the ship and disappear into a crowd of sailors and Marines. Mom's eyes welled up with tears of worry. Rhonda openly sobbed. I bit my lower lip hard to keep from crying. My father was the only one who spoke, his voice choked with emotion.

"Thank God our part of the war over there is finished," he said.

"I don't think you ever told me you had a brother killed in Nam," Fred said, bringing me back to the present.

"I don't think you ever asked."

Fred grunted. "Probably. Old habits are hard to break. We always said, 'You only need to know what you need to know.'"

"One more thing, Fred," I said. "Ask around about a black-market operator named Tobias Denton." I spelled the name out for him. "He was smuggling technology throughout Southeast Asia from the Seventies until a couple of years ago. See if your friends have anything on him."

"Is this a shopping list or what?" Fred grumbled.

"Please?" I said sweetly, with plenty of sugar and syrup.

"Okay. The first one shouldn't be hard to find out," he said. "The second one—I don't know. I'll ask around."

"Thanks, Fred."

"I'll let you know what I find out," Fred said. "Then you owe me some whiskey."

The line went dead.

I called Mike McCarty next.

"Hey, Moondoggie. Surf's up!"

"That's Lieutenant Moondoggie," Mike replied dryly. "And, yes, I know surf's up, but I'm stuck in this damn office talking to you. What do you want?"

"I thought I'd fill you in on what I learned from that Customs agent you spoke with," I said.

"Oh, do share," Mike said, pretending to yawn.

"Seems Customs believes our Thomas Danner is actually someone named Tobias Denton, a tech smuggler in Southeast Asia they've had an eye on for some time. Denton disappeared about a year before Danner showed up here."

"Do tell."

"And Denton turned up in the black market there not long after my brother and his friend, TD, were supposedly killed," I added.

"Supposedly?"

"Well, if Rhonda was right and Danner is TD …"

"That's all?" Mike still sounded bored, but I heard him scribbling notes.

"You got anything better?"

"Yeah, as a matter of fact, I do," Mike snorted. "My guys found some CCTV video showing Danner in Ms. White's hotel the night she died."

My hand gripped the telephone handset. "What?"

"Don't get too excited," Mike said. "It shows Danner went into the bar, had a drink, and left."

"And …?"

"And that's it, except …"

"Except? Don't toy with me, Mike."

"The same video shows Ms. White walking out of the bar and exiting the lobby shortly after Danner."

"How shortly?"

"Short enough for us to question Danner about it, but not short enough for us to link the two together."

"What did Danner say?"

"He says he went to the bar for a drink on his way home, as he does most nights," Mike said. "He lives on a boat in the marina next to the hotel. Said he didn't know the vict was staying there."

"And …?"

"My guys questioned a couple of the bartenders, and they confirmed he comes in most nights on his way back to his boat. That night, the guy tending bar said Danner had one quick drink and left. Didn't see him talk to anyone."

"Maybe Danner was waiting for Rhonda in the parking lot," I said. "Did you think of that?"

"No, Sherlock, it never occurred to me or any of my highly trained detectives," Mike sneered. "Of course, we did. We checked the parking lot video, which showed them both getting into their own cars in separate parts of the lot and driving off. No sign they were together or even knew each other."

I took a deep breath and blew it out slowly. "So, I guess you've crossed Danner off your suspects list?"

"Not necessarily," Mike said.

"Why's that?"

"When my guys talked to him," Mike said, "they said his mouth kept twitching."

☼

My last call was to Dick Sanders, the Customs agent.

"Why the hell do you have Tygard following me?" I demanded.

"And a fucking good morning to you, too, Brandt," Sanders replied.

"Well?"

"Well, what?"

"Why is Tygard tailing me?"

"What the hell makes you think he is?" Sanders said. "And, if he is, what makes you think I have anything to do with it?

"I spotted him this morning at the Veteran's Memorial on Mount Soledad," I said.

"Maybe he was watching the fucking sunrise."

"People go there to view the sunset, not the sunrise. Now drop the Bronx tough-guy act, Sanders," I said. "It isn't working. Now, why is Tygard following me?"

The line was quiet for several seconds before Sanders sighed.

"Because I can't." he said. "I'm a cop and it'd be a violation of your rights. As far as I'm concerned, Tygard is a private citizen and what he does is no concern of mine."

"He's an Israeli citizen," I said.

"So, he's an Israeli private citizen. He still has rights."

"Even as a spy?"

"Get a copy of the U.S. Constitution and read it, Brandt," Sanders said. "The Fourteenth Amendment. That equal protection under the law crap."

"Okay. So, why does he think I need to be followed? I've told you all I know."

"Because, Brandt, you have a habit of putting your nose in places it shouldn't be."

"The last time my nose was some place it shouldn't have been," I said, "you and an FBI agent put it there."

Sanders went quiet again. When he spoke again, his attitude was much nicer.

"Look, we don't know who else might be looking for Danner or Denton, or whatever the hell his real name is," he said. "We don't know if there is someone, but this guy has all the hallmarks of someone who's spent his life looking over his shoulder."

"He's a crook," I said. "Isn't that reason enough?"

"Possible," Sanders said. "Call it professional intuition, but Tygard and I both feel someone else is out there that Denton/Danner is afraid of. Whoever it is, he may be even more dangerous than Danner."

"So, you're using me as bait again?" I said. "Wait for this *mystery guy* to take me out so you can ID him and make the arrest?"

"Come on, Brandt, you know I don't work that way," Sanders said. "And neither does Tygard. You of all people should know that."

I let that sink in. The Mossad had a rep for assassinating people they considered a danger to Israel. But Tygard had never shown himself to be that cold blooded. In fact, he once saved my life. And Jo's, too.

I nodded as if Sanders could see it. "Okay, I guess I'll let Tygard be the good shepherd." I changed the subject. "Did you know Danner lives on a boat in a marina on Harbor Island?"

"We know," Sanders said, returning to his Bronx persona. "It's called the Suzanne. A sixty-five-foot ketch. He doesn't own it. Just leases it from the owner—or rather the owner's family. The owner is doing a dime stretch for stock fraud. Anyway, we suspect Danner plans to use it to take some of his illegal tech out of the country. I made a request to the Coast Guard, the Harbor Police, and our own marine unit to report any movements, but so far, he hasn't taken it out. You taking notes?"

"Yes, I am," I said.

"God, I hate reporters," Sanders said.

"I do, too," I told him.

"Background only, and you never learned this from me."

"Of course," I said. "Have you checked the boat out? I mean, gone aboard and checked it out?"

"No. As long as he stays tied up to the dock, we need probable cause to get a search warrant," Sanders said. "If he'd get underway, the Coast Guard could stop him for what they call a safety check and go aboard. Until then, we're stuck—unless …"

I didn't like how the line stayed quiet for such a long time. "Unless what?" I demanded.

Somehow at that moment, I knew I shouldn't have asked.

Chapter 16

"EXPLAIN TO ME AGAIN why you want *me* to do this?" I demanded.

We were parked on the main road on Harbor Island overlooking the marina. Tygard sat in the driver's seat of his compact sedan, and Dick Sanders sat next to him. I sat in the back, eyeing a ring of strange keys the Mossad agent had handed me.

"Because I can't do it," Sanders said. "If I got caught, it'd be an unwarranted search, a violation of the motherfucker's civil rights, and I'd be fired in a New York minute. Tygard can't do it because if he got caught, he'd be deported as an undesirable alien."

"And if I get caught?"

"You are distraught over the murder of your old family friend, and you wanted answers, but you weren't thinking right," Sanders said. "Most you'd get is a warning, maybe probation if Danner presses charges."

"*If* he presses charges?"

"He won't," Sanders assured me. "He wants to stay as far away from the legal system as he can."

"Isn't this what the FBI used to call a 'black bag job'?" I asked.

"They still do," Sanders said, "but the Bureau has better attorneys than we do."

"And you're sure you've got the right boat?" I asked. "This Suzanne?"

Sanders glanced at Tygard and scowled as he shook his head. "Yes, it's the boat Danner lives on. Now, are you finished asking questions?"

"No," I said. I held up the key ring. "What do I do with these?"

"They are called *bump keys*, Mr. Brandt," Tygard explained in his professorial voice. "They are used for picking locks. Now, I studied Danner's boat through my binoculars—" He held up a pair of large, German-made field glasses. "And he has the door to his main cabin secured with a hasp and a padlock. That key you are holding should fit it. The one next to it should fit the lock to the marina gate leading down to the dock. Insert the key into the lock and turn it to the right. It won't turn at first but keep applying pressure as you tap the back of the key with this." He handed me a flat strip of metal about five inches long with a rubber ball at the tip. "After a few taps, the key should turn and open the lock."

I studied the keys and the funny little hammer and asked, "Is this something from the Mossad bag of secret squirrel tricks?"

"Actually, I purchased it last night at a local hardware store," Tygard replied.

"Now have you finished with the fucking questions, Brandt?" Sanders demanded.

Slipping the keys and their hammer into my back pocket, I nodded, opened the door, and paused. "What am I looking for again?"

Sanders buried his head in his hands and shook it. "Anything unusual. Hidden compartments, strange documents, a military-grade supercomputer …"

"Just photograph the interior, Mr. Brandt," Tygard said, handing me a digital camera the size of a pack of cigarettes. "And good luck."

I slid the camera into the other back pocket of my white jeans. My light-weight shirt, left partly unbuttoned, sported a flowery, tropical Hawaiian theme. My shoes were brown Docksiders boat shoes, and I wore my dark aviator sunglasses. A plastic bucket and brush finished my ensemble. I looked like any other boat bum headed down to the dock to work on his boat. Or so I hoped.

Reaching the marina gate, I glanced around. No one was about, so I inserted the key and tried turning it. As Tygard said, it didn't move. Keeping pressure on the key, I tapped its butt end a few times with the little hammer, and it turned, unlocking the gate. I fought the urge to glance back at Tygard and Sanders and raise my arms in victory.

The Suzanne, a sixty-five-foot ketch moored at the end of a finger dock, had a black hull and white trim. Her deck was varnished teak, as was the low-slung cabin. A towering main mast was stepped forward of the cabin, and the smaller mizzen stood forward of the helm with its large, old-fashioned wooden-spoked wheel, also varnished. I'm not much of a sailor, but even I could see the Suzanne was what old salts call *yar*.

Before stepping aboard the Suzanne, I glanced around again. It was mid-morning on a weekday, and the marina was empty. The liveaboards had gone off to their land-lubbing jobs, and the sunshine sailors were still sitting at their desks ashore dreaming of weekend sailing. Tygard assured me Danner had already left for his office.

The ketch heeled toward the dock as I stepped aboard. I paused, holding my breath, waiting for a voice to call out from the cabin. But as the vessel was locked from the outside, I needn't have worried. Stepping over to the cabin door, I hunched down, inserted the key Tygard told me to use, and repeated the bumping exercise. A loud click, and the padlock popped open.

The Suzanne's below decks were as elegant as her topside, with varnished teak bulkheads, countertops, and a midship dining table. Portholes and wall lamps all gleamed with polished brass. A kitchenette with stove, refrigerator, and sink sat forward of the dining table. Opposite was a combination head and shower. The bench behind the table could convert into a bunk. The main bedroom was far forward in the fo'c'sle. A shoreline brought in electricity and, judging from the telephone in the main lounge, phone service as well.

All told, the Suzanne made my little bungalow look like a dump.

I took out the digital camera and began snapping shots. As I moved forward shooting pictures, I opened and examined every cabinet and compartment. I stamped on the deck and knocked on bulkheads, listening for the dull hollow sound of a hidden compartment. The only technology I found was what one would expect on a sea-going vessel— a marine radio, a GPS receiver sitting above the chart table, and a mounted EPRIB device that automatically sent a distress signal in case of sinking. A small color television/VCR combo hung on the bulkhead above the dining table.

The only anomaly was a hammerless .38 caliber revolver I found in a drawer next to the main bunk. I opened the cylinder and found it empty. There were no loose or boxed shells in the drawer, or anywhere else on the boat. If Danner were planning to use that pistol for self-defense, he'd better be good at bluffing in poker.

I finished photographing the boat and stuck the camera back into my rear pocket. As I turned to leave, I heard voices coming from the dock. My mouth went dry as the voices crept closer. Slipping over to a porthole, I peeked outside. Two men were walking toward the Suzanne and, as she was the only boat tied up at the end of the dock, it was obvious she was their destination. I ducked as they approached the boat, held my breath, and prayed.

"Ahoy, Mr. Danner!" yelled one of the men. "Mr. Danner, you aboard?"

As they waited for an answer, they talked quietly amongst themselves. "Mr. Danner has been living aboard the Suzanne for two years now. I'm sure he would tell you how much he likes it here." The man who I now guessed to be the marina manager called out again. "Ahoy, Mr. Danner. You home?"

The Suzanne heeled to starboard as someone—I assumed the marina manager—stepped aboard. I had left the padlock on the deck next to the hatch, and the hasp opened. If the manager saw that, he would realize someone was aboard. I glanced around the boat for some place to hide should he open the door and peek inside.

As his footsteps grew closer to the cabin, I slunk back through the boat and slipped into the head. It wasn't the first time I took cover in such a facility. During a mortar attack in El Salvador, I once dove face first into a slit trench latrine. The Suzanne's head was much nicer, but I still held my breath just as I did back then.

"Mr. Danner?" The footsteps paused. A shoe squeaked topside, and the footsteps receded. "Well, I guess he's already gone to his office," the manager said.

The Suzanne rocked as the manager leapt onto the dock. As their footsteps moved away, I slipped out of the head and heard the manager say, "Funny, I thought I saw him climbing aboard only a few minutes ago. Must've been somebody else on another boat. These old eyes aren't what they used to be, you know."

I waited a full fifteen minutes before poking my head out of the cabin door and looking around. Seeing no one about, I climbed back onto the deck, closed the hatch, snapped the padlock in place, and left the Suzanne.

"Well?"

I closed the car door, handed the camera back to Tygard, and shook my head.

"Well, nothing," I said. "Nada. Zilch. The Suzanne is as gorgeous on the inside as she is on the outside."

"We didn't send you to do an interior décor review," Sanders growled. "Did you find anything unusual?"

"No," I said. "Nothing out of the ordinary. No secret compartments I could find. No tech other than what you'd normally find on a boat. The only thing I found unusual was an unloaded revolver in a bedroom drawer. There were no bullets for it anywhere."

Tygard cleared his throat.

"What?"

"Oh, oh, nothing," he said. "Nothing at all, Mr. Brandt. Just a bit of mucus buildup. Allergies."

In the rearview mirror, I saw the Mossad agent steal a glance at Sanders, but I wasn't sure. I leaned forward to see the photo he was looking at, but Tygard switched off the little display screen and placed it in the glove compartment. A touch of fear and suspicion rushed through me, but I put it off to the dying ebb of adrenalin in my system.

"Good day, Mr. Brandt," Tygard said. "Thank you once again for your services."

"Yeah, thanks," added Sanders. "Don't let the bed bugs bite."

As I got out and watched them drive off, I had a hunch there was something more to my suspicions than losing my adrenalin high.

Chapter 17

THAT NIGHT, JO INVITED Jack and me to dinner at her apartment. As soon as I let him out of his carrier, Jack ran into the hallway, his claws skittering on the wooden floor. A moment later, he came swooshing out of the hall like an Olympic tobogganer and thumped into the back of the couch. Without a pause, he was back on his four paws and, with a shake of his head, headed back up the hallway to repeat the exercise.

Jo and I watched Jack as we sipped Merlot. I asked, "What's for grub?"

"I decided on Italian 'grub,' as you put it," said Jo, sauntering into the kitchen.

"Pizza?"

I could almost hear her eyes roll. "When I make Italian, I make Italian," she said. "Cacio e pepe, a tomato, basil, cucumber panzanella, and chicken cacciatore."

"And for dessert?" I asked.

She gave me a sultry glance. "Me—if you play your cards right."

Another clattering of claws, a swoosh, and a thump.

"What's Jack eating?"

"Fresh salmon."

"You spoil him," I said.

"I spoil you both," she replied.

Dinner was a feast. For someone who pretty much subsists on microwavable food and takeout, any home-cooked meal was a feast. But Jo outdid herself with the Italian cuisine. Afterward, we sat on the couch sharing a second bottle of Merlot and watching the city lights dancing across the bay. Jack, worn out from playing and with a tummy full of fresh fish, snoozed in his personal bed.

"Where did you learn to cook Italian?" I asked.

"My mother's Italian," she said. "I never told you that?"

"You're part Italian?" I looked her up and down. "With blonde hair and blue eyes?"

"My grandparents came from northern Italy," Jo explained. "You've never been to Italy?"

I shook my head. "I've never been to Europe."

Jo looked at me, astonished. "With all the reporting you've done outside the U.S., you never went to Europe?"

"Closest I came was the Middle East during Desert Storm."

"Well, genetically, northern Italy is more Northern European than southern Italy because of centuries of invasions and occupations," she said. "My grandparents grew up near the Dolomites—part of the Italian Alps. A lot of fighting happened there during the First World War. When it ended, my grandparents came to the States."

"Huh, war—the great mover of people," I said.

We remained silent for a while, each of us lost in our own histories of conflict and horror. Jo broke the silence.

"So, how was your day?" she asked. "Did you get much writing done?"

"Not really," I said, feeling a pang of guilt for not working on my new book with a deadline looming. "I broke into a yacht instead."

Jo chuckled. "You what?"

"I broke into Danner's boat and searched it."

Jo said nothing. I glanced at her and saw the icicles in her pale blue eyes that gave her the nickname "Cold as Ice Rice."

"Tell me you're kidding," she said. "Please, for all that is holy, *tell me you are fucking kidding.*"

I looked at her, confused. "No, no, I'm not," I stammered. "Sanders and Tygard—"

Jo jumped to her feet and stood over me. "Oh, my God, those two again? What? If they asked you to jump off a bridge, you'd jump?"

"You're sounding like my mother," I said, standing.

"Well, maybe that's what you need," she blurted, "a mommy to take care of you, to keep you from getting hurt. Do you remember what happened the last time you tried to break into some place? You almost got yourself killed."

"I was trying to rescue you," I said in my defense.

"And you almost got us *both* killed."

"There was no chance of me getting killed—"

"You think Danner killed your friend Rhonda!" Jo threw up her hands. "If he killed her, why the hell wouldn't he kill you?"

"Well, he wasn't even there—"

We heard a scamper down the hall. Jack stood outside the bedroom door, eyes wide, ears tilted back, fur upright. He looked at us and dashed back into the bedroom, presumably to hide under the bed—which was what I felt like doing.

Jo turned away, hugged herself with one arm and, with the other arm propped on it, rubbed her forehead. "Peter," she said, her voice now gentle. "If you'd been caught, you could have been arrested and sent to prison …"

"But I wasn't. I didn't even come close to being caught." A minor lie.

"But you could've! And then what?" she demanded, her voice rising again. "What about Jack? What about me?" She waved her hand between the two of us. "What about *us*?"

Jo paced the floor before facing me. "Look, Peter, I know things haven't been always smooth between us—"

"Like you dumping me for another man?" I regretted saying it before I even finished saying it.

The icicles came back to her eyes, but they soon melted. She nodded slowly.

"Yes, like that," she said. "And like me not wanting to get married again." She gestured toward me. "And like you being afraid of commitment after your first marriage. Let's not forget that."

Touché. I had to give her that.

"But I like what we have now," she said. "I don't want to lose it. I don't want to lose *you*. I have too much invested in us …"

"So do I," I said, stepping up to her.

"We both do," she agreed. "So why take stupid chances that can get you killed or something? If we're going to screw this up, let us do it on our own."

I took her in my arms. "We're not going to screw this up."

I kissed her. It took a while before she kissed me back. Afterward, we just stood there, holding each other. Warm tears fell on my shoulder.

Jack peeked around the corner of the bedroom door and mewed.

"It's all right, Jack," I said. "We're all right." I looked at Jo. "We are, aren't we?"

Jo nodded and kissed me. I didn't hesitate to return the favor. From the hallway came a clatter of claws, a swoosh, followed by a thud. We turned and Jack leapt on the back of the couch, purring.

"So," I said, "am I still getting dessert?"

When we got home the next morning, I fed Jack breakfast. Seeing me opening a can, he realized breakfast would be his standard fare and not something freshly hauled from the sea. His tail flicked in anger, but he ate it anyway. I needed to work on the new book, but it was early still, the sun only beginning to warm the streets, and I figured I had time for a quick run. After changing into running shorts and shoes, I decided to check my email before heading out. One was from Fred Danbury. Sent the night before, it read: "Lunch at that Mex eatery I like. Noon. FD."

With my spare time now evaporated, I gave up my idea of a run. After a shower and a shave, I sat back at the computer and wrote until it was time to meet Fred.

Chapter 18

THE "MEX EATERY," AS Fred called it, was a restaurant called Margarita's. Located on Ocean Beach's main drag, Newport Avenue, two blocks from the beach, it stood in the middle of the little community's alternative culture scene. A throwback to the 1960s, OB thus far had avoided the gentrification that transformed San Diego from a fishing harbor and Navy town into a metropolis. Antique stores lined the street alongside used-clothing shops, health-food stores, coffee houses, bars, and even old-fashioned smoke shops. Aging hippies with thinning gray hair tied back in ponytails walked its streets along with the young and the beautiful of the latest generation. Sailors from the nearby Navy bases came on their lunch breaks to ogle the girls in their next-to-nothing bikinis, with businessmen in suits and ties right behind them. To call OB quaint would be an exaggeration.

Music blared from outdoor bars, competing with the roar of low-flying airliners taking off from Lindbergh Field, and squawking flocks of parrots that somehow got lost in migration and took roost on this side of the border. It was a loud, sometimes boisterous throwback, and I called it home.

Fred stood waiting for me outside Margarita's, wearing dark, wrap-around sunglasses, puffing on one of his black cigarillos, and trying to not be too obvious as he eyed the glistening parade of oiled, nubile bodies heading toward the beach. Entranced by the exhibit of young flesh, he didn't spot me walking up behind him.

"You're losing your touch, Fred," I said, sticking my finger in his back like a pistol.

"No, I'm not," he said, still admiring the scene. "I saw you walking up in that window reflection."

He nodded toward the window in Margarita's storefront, where I saw my reflection clearly displayed.

"And you better get that finger out of my back, or you'll need to have it sewn back on." Before I could move my hand, he drew a knife from a pocket and flipped it open. He closed it just as quickly, his thin, downwardly angled mustache stretched straight by a grin. "How ya doing, Petey?" He clamped an arm around my shoulders, tossed his cigarillo into the street, and led me into the restaurant. "You hungry? I'm famished. By the way, you're paying."

Fred flirted with the plump waitress as he ordered a beer and enchiladas in his Texan-accented Spanish. My Spanish was better than his, but I still ordered coffee and machaca con huevos in English.

"So, Fred, what brings you here from Orange County?" I asked. "Getting away from Doris again?"

"You're damn right I am," he said, shaking his head. "Swear to God, that broad drives me crazy. Like being married without the benefits—not that I'd want to have benefits with her. You've seen her."

Doris was his secretary and the only other employee of his travel agency. Middle-aged, somewhat plump, she appeared to have drawn a perpetual growl on her face with lipstick. "She's very protective of you," I said.

The waitress brought my coffee and Fred's beer. He took an angry swig. "Do I look like I need protecting? I've got two ex-wives and I'm not looking for a third." He took another swig and changed the subject. "Besides, I came here with some info on that NIS guy you asked me about."

"And to get away from Doris," I chided.

"And to get away from Doris," he agreed, nodding. "But you're buying me lunch because of the stuff I got on the NIS guy."

"Okay, shoot."

"The guy's name is Bradwell. Nelson Bradwell," Fred said. "I talked with an old colleague who was chief of station in Saigon for the Company when I flew for Air America. He knew Bradwell. Wasn't too impressed with him."

"Why not?" I asked.

"NIS wasn't as professional back then as they are now," Fred explained. "I should say, as NCIS is now. In the Sixties and Seventies, NIS used a lot of amateurs, former cops and such who signed on as temporary contractors. Not many people wanted to sign up to go to Nam. Hell, guys were dressing up in drag to avoid going there. So, NIS took whoever they could get—just luck of the draw. Some were good, some decent, and some—well, my buddy put Bradwell in the last category."

"And yet he became NIS station chief in Saigon?"

The waitress came with our food, and Fred waited to answer until she set the plates down and left.

"By virtue of attrition," Fred continued, a forkful of enchilada in his mouth. I took a bite of my machaca while he chewed and swallowed. "He stayed longer than anyone else. Most of the agents left when their one-year contract expired, but Bradwell held on until the fall of Saigon."

I did the math. "Bradwell was already station chief when my brother died in 1972," I said. "So, he'd already been there a while by then. And he stayed on with the NIS in Nam until Saigon fell in 1975?" Fred nodded as he chewed another mouthful of enchilada. "He must've been happy there. But why?"

Fred swallowed hard and swigged some more beer. "My buddy says he heard Bradwell ended up making NIS a career," he said. "That surprised my buddy because in Nam no one seemed to trust him, not even his own agents."

"Doesn't sound like someone who'd rise through the ranks easily," I said as I shoveled more machaca into my mouth.

"You know how it is, Peter," Fred said. "Shit floats to the top in some bureaucracies. I knew some great people in the Company, and a lot of dumb fucks. Always seemed the dumb fucks were better at playing the promotion game—currying favors, stealing credit, and passing the blame. Probably the same at NCIS."

I nodded. It was the same in journalism. The best ones became discouraged and left the profession while the jerks stayed and played their games.

"What else?" I asked.

"About Bradwell?" I nodded again. Fred frowned. "That's it. My buddy hasn't seen or heard of him in years. Probably retired somewhere by now."

We finished our meals, and I paid the bill. It wasn't much information, but at least now I had a name. I figured that was worth the price of lunch. As we stepped out of Margarita's, an airliner roared overhead. Fred slipped on his wraparounds, lit a cigar, and watched the jet as it winged over the ocean. I'm not psychic or an empath, but I sensed a strong sadness in Fred.

"Doing much flying these days, Fred?" I asked.

He looked at me. "You mean like the old times?" He frowned and shook his head. "No more wars for this old flyboy. No flying either, for that matter. Lost my license." He tapped his chest. "Ticker problems."

Every writer goes through periods when they feel the words no longer flow. It's frightening, like you've lost your identity, your reason for being. I understood how a career flyer like Fred must feel.

"Sorry to hear that, Fred," I said. "I know how much you love flying."

Fred shrugged and gave me a sly smile. "'Oh! I have slipped the surly bonds of Earth, and danced the skies on laughter-silvered wings …'"

I added the concluding line of the poem known by all airmen. "'Put out my hand and touched the face of God.'"

Patting me on the shoulder, Fred laughed and said, "Hell, Petey, closest I ever got to God was the Mile High Club."

He glanced at the sky again. "You know, I think I'm going to go for a walk along the beach, catch me some rays, and breathe in that salt air. Take care of yourself now, partner, you hear?"

Fred turned and walked away, glancing skyward at another passing jet. He reminded me of a bird with a broken wing, unable to fly, stuck on the ground, waiting for the inevitable predator. For Fred Danbury, the predator was death itself.

Chapter 19

AS I WALKED BACK to my bungalow, I called Dick Sanders.

"What is it?" he answered.

"And good afternoon to you," I said.

"I'm too busy for pleasantries, Brandt," Sanders said. "What do you want?"

"Do you know of an NIS—NCIS now—agent named Bradwell, Nelson Bradwell?" I asked.

"What do you think," Sanders replied, "all us feds get together on Friday night and play poker?"

"Do you?"

"Are you kidding? We barely talk to each other," Sanders said. "Everyone knows those Navy squids cheat at cards. So, if you don't have anything else—"

The line went quiet, then Sanders asked, "You said Bradwell, right?"

"Bradwell," I confirmed. "Nelson Bradwell. You know him?"

"Hold on." I heard a desk drawer creak open and what sounded like rummaging as Sanders murmured to himself. "Bradwell … Bradwell … Here it is …" He paused before reading from what I assumed was a business card. "Nelson Bradwell, special agent in charge, Southwest Field Office, Building 57, Naval Station San Diego … I remember now. It was my first case here, liaising with NCIS and DEA on a case involving some sailors smuggling narcotics on the side."

"He still there?" I asked.

"How the fuck do I know?" Sanders answered. "That was years ago. I was just a young pup of an agent."

I couldn't imagine Sanders as a young pup of anything, but I didn't say so. "That business card you're reading from have a phone number?"

"Yep." Sanders read it to me. His voice grew suspicious. "What the hell is this all about, Brandt? What's this guy to you?"

"He had something to do with how my brother was killed in Nam," I explained. "He was the NIS head of station or something in Saigon. I want to talk to him and find out what happened."

"If this has any fucking thing to do with Danner, you'd better keep me advised," Sanders warned.

"Sure thing," I said and ended the call.

Jack must have heard me approaching. As I walked up to my front door, I heard him howl and paw at the door. He appeared at the window, glared at me, and jumped down to scratch the door some more. When I entered, he circled my legs twice before trotting into the kitchen to show me his kibble bowl was low. I added more to the bowl, then dialed the NCIS number Sanders gave me.

The female receptionist who answered denied a Nelson Bradwell worked for NCIS. I told her I knew he had once been agent in charge of the agency's Southwest Field Office. That gave her pause. She put me on hold. When she came back on the line, she said, "Yes, Mr. Bradwell *was* agent in charge, but that was some time ago. He's retired now."

"Do you have any contact information for him?" I asked. "Or know where he retired to?"

"I'm sorry, no," she said.

I tried tugging at her heartstrings and told her my story about doing a family history and how Bradwell might have information on how my brother died in Vietnam since he had been the NIS station chief there.

"Sir, we never give out information on any of our personnel, active or retired, living or dead," she said. "That is our policy. Goodbye."

The line went dead. It must be government policy to have the heartstrings removed from federal employees.

I sat at my computer and started a web search for any mention of Nelson Bradwell. High-ranking federal workers rarely put themselves out to pasture when they retire. Like former members of Congress, they hold a wealth of marketable knowledge and experience that can be useful for certain corporations. They almost always hang out their own shingle. That usually gets some press notice, even if nothing more than a publicity release announcing their new endeavor. I came up with zilch.

My cell phone rang. Jo.

"What'cha doing, stud muffin?" she asked.

"That's Mr. Stud Muffin to you," I replied.

"Okay, what are you doing, Mr. Stud Muffin?"

I told her about my meeting with Fred Danbury and the information he gave me about Bradwell. "I'm searching the web for any information on him."

"And?"

"Getting nothing," I said.

"Of course not," she said. "You need to do a background check."

"Sure," I said. "And how do I get access to the information I'd need for that?"

"You could buy me dinner tonight," Jo said. "Some place nice. Like Top of the Cove in La Jolla."

"You can do a background check on Bradwell?" I asked, incredulous.

"I do background checks for my clients all the time," she said. "Some of them do classified work for the government. They need to know who they're hiring. Tell me more about him."

I told her everything I'd learned about Bradwell, his tour in Vietnam in the Seventies, his stint as agent in charge of the NCIS Southwest Regional Office.

"Okay," she said. "I've got a meeting to go to in a few minutes, but I'll get it started. Pick me up at seven."

The open terrace at the Top of the Cove in La Jolla boasted one of the most spectacular ocean views in the city—perhaps anywhere in Southern California. Even though we missed the sunset, the dark, cloudless sky provided us with an astounding panoramic view of moonlight glittering upon a nearly flat sea. Stars fell from the heavens like a curtain and rested on the distant horizon. Ships and other vessels added their flickering lights to the glitter, and to the south, another brightly lit cruise ship steamed toward Mexican waters.

And yet, the view paled next to Jo.

Sensitive about the shrapnel scars on her hip, Jo never wore short dresses. Feminine business suits or simple jeans were her uniform since leaving the Army. That night, though, she wore a long, simmering evening dress that hugged the curves of her figure and revealed a generous décolletage. Below the hem of the dress, stiletto-heeled pumps heightened the allure of her shapely athletic legs. Murmured conversations among the diners paused as the maître 'd escorted us to our table.

We both opted for the lobster, though Jo worried about dripping butter sauce on her dress. I told her I would lick it off if she did. She rolled her eyes and said, "That's my stud muffin."

"Mr. Stud Muffin," I corrected.

Any information about Nelson Bradwell waited until we finished eating.

"So, your spook friend was right," Jo said, sipping an after-meal *digestif*. "Bradwell had an extensive tour of duty in Saigon. Looks like he enjoyed himself too much."

"People call it 'going native,' " I said. "Sometimes happens with foreign correspondents. You fall in love with a culture and start adopting its lifestyle, mannerisms, and such."

"I don't think so," Jo said, slowly shaking her head. "I think he had no place else to go."

My eyes narrowed. "What do you mean?"

"He was sort of the black sheep of a well-off family," Jo explained. "Born with the proverbial 'silver spoon' in his mouth. Daddy was a successful lawyer and big into state politics, and his mother taught at a prestigious private university. His brother followed his father into law and politics, while his sister became a surgeon—all thanks to those alumni legacy acceptances that rich kids get. But Bradwell did none of that. He became a cop."

"Maybe he was rebellious," I said. "Wanted to prove himself on his own."

Jo shrugged. "Anyway, he joined the Orange County Sheriff's Department, where he ran patrol and later joined the bomb squad. After a few years, he left suddenly—suddenly enough to raise eyebrows."

"Like he was given a choice?" I asked. Jo nodded. "Resign or be fired—or worse, prosecuted?"

"Maybe," Jo said. "There were several citizen complaints filed against him, none of them made public. That's not so unusual. Happens a lot with cops, particularly patrol cops. Suspects try to get even with the officers who arrest them by claiming they used excessive force. Even so, he had quite a few and they stopped when he joined the bomb squad."

"Because he wasn't on the street anymore," I said. "Like they took him off patrol to stop the complaints?"

"Probably," Jo agreed. "Anyway, whatever it was, it wasn't enough to keep him from being hired by NCIS—I mean NIS."

"Fred told me that NIS had a less professional reputation in the past than it does now," I said. "The agents were independent contractors—ex-cops, but not necessarily trained as federal agents." I sipped my drink. "If he spent so much time overseas, I take it he wasn't married."

"Divorced," she said. "Early in his sheriff's career. The marriage didn't last a year, and the divorce papers are under seal."

"So, someone—Bradwell or his wife—didn't want certain information made public," I said.

"My guess is Bradwell," Jo said. "Probably involved spousal abuse. Doesn't look good for that kind of information to come out when a cop testifies in a trial."

Nor would it be helpful for an officer facing a disciplinary hearing over allegations of police abuse, I thought. "Okay, after his time with the OC Sheriff's and his stint in Vietnam, what happened?"

"He stayed in the agency and rose through the ranks," Jo said, "most often with the help of his family's political connections. Held several overseas posts—the Middle East, Rota, Spain, Sasebo, Japan—anywhere the Navy posted personnel. In fact, he seemed to prefer working overseas.

His sunset tour was agent in charge in San Diego, as we already knew."

Jo sipped her drink before continuing. "But he seemed to have done well financially, more than you would expect someone to do on a GS salary. Bought and sold property. Traveled a lot. There was a rumor he inherited some money when his parents died, but I couldn't find evidence of that."

I scratched my ear and shook my head. I had to hand it to Jo. She knew her work. "I'm amazed you could learn that much from a background check in such a short time," I said.

"Well, it helped that I used to date the guy who's now the agent in charge of the NCIS San Diego office," Jo said, smiling. "He worked with Bradwell and didn't care much for him."

I remembered what Fred said about Bradwell's own team members in Saigon not trusting him. Then my own distrust issues rose. "What'd you have to give this guy for all this information?"

Jo glanced at me sideways, a sly smile playing on her lips. "Oh, only a chance at rekindling old embers."

I didn't respond. The lump in my throat wouldn't let me.

"Oh, come on, Peter," Jo said, reaching across the table and touching my hand. "I'm joking. He's married with three kids, one in college. I think he cooperated because he secretly hopes we turn up something on Bradwell."

I held her hand and smiled. I liked the way she said "we."

Chapter 20

JO'S BACKGROUND CHECK ON Bradwell turned up a phone number and address in Laguna Beach. I called the number twice that day, each time leaving a message about my family history ruse. Neither call was returned. No surprise there. Most people prefer to ignore their past, especially when that past has skeletons best left in the closet.

The next morning, after feeding Jack and filling his kibble bowl, I headed north on the I-5 for the seventy-nine-mile drive to Laguna Beach. The rush-hour traffic had thinned, and I made good time, barreling past Camp Pendleton into Orange County. Being in no hurry, I dropped off the freeway and took the scenic route through the small harbor town of Dana Point. The town's namesake, Richard Henry Dana, Jr., described this area as the most romantic part of the West Coast in his seagoing memoir, *Two Years Before the Mast*.

But after spending two years on a merchant sailing ship, enduring two transits of Cape Horn's tumultuous seas, as well as a ship captain who enjoyed flogging sailors, I guess purgatory would look romantic.

Laguna Beach was once known for its surfing and its artist colony, but gentrification drove all but the most stubborn surfers and artisans out, replacing them with expensive homes owned by people for whom an ocean sunset and the crash of waves were nothing more than the backdrop for a three-martini happy hour. Despite being the family's black sheep, I figured Bradwell inherited some of its wealth if he could afford to live there. That, or the retirement benefits for federal employees are far too generous.

Bradwell's home wasn't as large as some I've seen—after all, I worked in Palm Springs for several years, where the wealthy keep massive mansions as winter retreats. A red Spanish-tiled roof topped two stories of white imitation adobe, with a balcony on the second story that offered a lovely view of the sun setting into the ocean. Neatly trimmed hedgerows surrounded an immaculate lawn and provided privacy from prying eyes. To one side, a cement driveway led to a two-door garage in front of which sat a late model Lexus. Yes, Nelson Bradwell had done himself well.

A middle-aged Hispanic housecleaner with suspicious eyes answered my knock. "*Sí?*"

"*Por favor, me gustaría hablar con el Señor Bradwell*," I said.

Her eyes brightened at my Spanish, but she replied, "*Lo lamento. El Señor Bradwell no recibirá visitas hoy.*"

Bradwell was not seeing visitors, but I persisted. I told her my supposed reason for wanting to see Bradwell. "*Mi familia estaría muy agradecida. La muerte de mi hermano en Vietnam fue un gran choque,*" I added, pulling on her heartstrings. *My family would be very grateful. My brother's death in Vietnam was quite a shock.*

The woman's face dropped and her eyes watered. She touched my arm.

"*Entiendo el dolor de tu familia. Perdí a mi hijo en ese atentado en Beirut,*" she said, dabbing a tear from her eye. *I understand your family's pain. I lost my son in that bombing in Beirut.*

I touched her arm and offered my condolences. In 1983, terrorists detonated a bomb outside a building housing American Marines, soldiers, and sailors serving as peacekeepers in Beirut during the Lebanese Civil War. Over two hundred of them died.

She bade me to wait and closed the door. Her soft footsteps retreated on a hardwood floor. Minutes later, heavier footsteps approached. The door swung open, and I stood face-to-face with Nelson Bradwell.

He stood a bit taller than me and much wider. His tan face sagged with age but his hair, though white, was still full and made his tan look deeper. Dull, gray-blue eyes peered at me, void of any of the cleaning lady's sympathy.

"Now, look here, Brandt, I got your phone messages, but I have no—"

I held the photograph of Keith, Rhonda, and Tommy Dykstra in front of his face. "This is my brother, Keith Brandt," I said tapping his image. "That's his fiancée, Rhonda." I tapped Dykstra's image. "You should remember this guy, Tommy Dykstra."

"I don't—"

"I spoke with one of my brother's former battalion members," I said, skirting around naming Colonel Candee. "He told me how NCIS—back then NIS—arranged with his battalion commander to give Dykstra a pass to Saigon to meet with your agents. The battalion commander insisted Keith go with him because Tommy was such a screwup. According to my source, they died in a bombing in Saigon, and afterward you—the NIS station chief—and this battalion commander ordered Keith's lieutenant to say they died in the firefight at the Da Nang airfield. All I want to know, Mr. Bradwell, is what the hell really happened to my brother?"

Bradwell worked his mouth as he looked at the photo, then back at me. His dull eyes narrowed, and he said, "You got ID?"

I pulled out my wallet and showed him my driver's license. Showing him my press credentials would only make him slam the door. He took a pair of black-rimmed reading glasses from his shirt pocket, slipped them on, and studied my license. Then he studied the photo again, his mouth still pursing and unpursing. Finally, he handed the photo back to me and pocketed his reading glasses.

"It's been a long time," he said, "but I'll see what I can remember."

Bradwell beckoned me inside with a jerk of his head and walked away, leaving me to close the door. He led me into a living room lined with wood paneling and filled with over-stuffed leather furniture. Photographs covered the paneled walls, showing him receiving awards or posing with pre-sumably important people. A couple of black-and-white pics showed a much younger Bradwell in Vietnam, wearing combat fatigues and sidearm, and carrying an M16 rifle.

I stopped and studied a color photo of Bradwell beaming as he posed with a strung-up marlin. A small fishing village sat in the background. Colorful opened-deck, single-masted boats rested on the beach, their sails furled, and nets strung out to dry. Beyond the boats I could see a modest cantina with log walls and roof, and a sign that read, Te Mana. I smiled at the memories it invoked. I knew the place well.

Sometimes it's better to warm a person up with small talk before starting the interview, so I asked, "You sport-fish?"

"When I can," Bradwell said. He poured himself a drink without offering me one.

"Where'd you catch this one?" I asked. "It's a beauty."

Bradwell hesitated. "It's a little fishing village in Mexico no gringos have ever heard of," he said. "I've got a little cabin up in the mountains. My private getaway."

My interest perked up. "Mexico?"

"Yeah, why?"

I shook my head. "This your cabin?" I asked, pointing to a picture of Bradwell standing on the porch of a rustic cabin surrounded by thick jungle growth. Bradwell wore khaki shorts and a tank top, held a drink in one hand and a much-too-young-for-him girl in the other.

"Yeah," he answered. He glanced at his watch. "Look, can we get on with this? I have a tee time at noon."

With another head jerk, Bradwell motioned me out to his backyard patio. With one last glance at the marlin photo, I followed him out, wondering why he had already lied to me.

Chapter 21

BRADWELL LED ME TO a patio table and lowered himself into a chair with a grunt. He sipped his drink, staring at some spot in the yard as he searched his memory.

"Tommy Dykstra, yeah, I remember the kid," he said with a tone devoid of fondness. "Dumbass kid. His CO said he was a real Sad Sack, always in trouble for something."

"Why did your agents want to meet with him in Saigon?" I asked.

My question seemed to disturb his thoughts. "Hmm? Oh, yeah. Well, we'd been investigating a black-market operation. Equipment, food, and other supplies disappeared from warehouses—both ours and ARVN's. That's the Army of the Republic of Vietnam. We'd ship the stuff to them, and it'd disappear, sometimes showing up in the hands of the NVA. That's the North Vietnam Army."

I grew up with the Vietnam War and understood the acronyms but said nothing.

"Tommy was involved?" I asked. "How?"

"Yeah, well, that's what we wanted to know," Bradwell said. He took another sip. "A couple of my agents worked the case and stumbled onto this Dykstra kid. Caught him trying to buy some drugs. But when they arrested him, he told them he could give them some bigger fish to fry if they let him go."

That sounded like Tommy, I thought. Lemieux and Alexander, Keith's platoon mates, said Tommy was always running some kind of scam.

"By 'bigger fish to fry' you mean the black-market operation?" I asked. Bradwell nodded. "How would some young, nobody Marine recently landed in Nam get involved with something like that?"

Bradwell chuckled as he took another sip of his cocktail. "He sure wasn't the mastermind, I'll tell you that," he said. "This Dykstra kid was just a small turd in a big sewer. He started working in his battalion's supply company. We figured someone in that company got involved in the black market during an earlier deployment, and once he was back in-country, he started up again."

"You don't know who?"

"We didn't have a clue," Bradwell said. "He wouldn't tell my agents until he had a deal. Of course, we check the records of everyone in that supply company to see who'd been in-country before, but there were like five or six suspects—too many to narrow down quickly."

"What was Tommy's role in this operation?"

"He would fly back and forth between Da Nang and Saigon as a sort of courier, delivering the stolen goods to the marketeers and bringing back the payment. But the little prick did a little freelancing on his own, too, picking up drugs in Saigon and taking them back to Da Nang to sell to the jarheads. That's how my agents stumbled onto him. The kid was scared stiff. He told my people he knew stuff about the black market, but like I said, he wouldn't give up any real info until he had a deal." Bradwell chuckled again. "Must've been in trouble with the law before he joined up. He knew all about working deals."

"So, you let him go back to Da Nang?"

"My agents sent him back with a list of information they wanted," Bradwell said, nodding. "Standard practice with informants, right? Give them a test, see what they can give you. Anyway, they arranged to meet him again in Saigon two weeks later when he made his next courier run. Only his battalion commander got wind of his going to Saigon and figured he was skylarking and confined him to the base. Dykstra got word to us, so my agents talked with his CO and convinced him to let him go. He agreed to give Dykstra a pass to Saigon *only* if your brother went with him to keep an eye on him. He figured the kid would take a hike or something."

"So, that's how Keith became involved?" I asked.

"Who? Oh, yeah, your brother," Bradwell said. "No, no. He wasn't involved with anything the Dykstra kid was up to, if that's what you're thinking. He wouldn't have gone to Saigon if not ordered to." Bradwell shook his head. "Your brother was collateral damage, that's all."

Dismissing Keith's death as "collateral damage" raised my hackles. Yet, I was flooded with relief. Keith hadn't been involved in anything illegal, and he hadn't deserted. He was in the wrong place at the wrong time. *Collateral damage.*

I swallowed hard and said, "Tell me what happened in Saigon."

Bradwell stuck a cigarette in his mouth, removed an old Zippo lighter, flipped it open with a flourish, and lit his smoke.

"Anyway, my agents were to meet up with the kid in this Saigon dive, only they couldn't contact him until he ditched your brother. Eventually, your brother left the bar. Maybe he got bored or mad at the other kid, or something." Bradwell shrugged. "Of course, we had the bar under surveillance inside and out, so we saw him leave. That's when the first bomb went off. Your brother turned around and ran back in, I guess, to help his buddy. Then came the second blast. Your brother, Dykstra, and both of my agents in the bar were killed. That's what happened, Brandt."

I became lost in my own thoughts for a moment. *If only Keith hadn't played hero and gone back for Tommy. If only ... Life was full of 'if onlies.' But that was Keith, big brother to everyone.*

Bradwell glanced at me. "You okay?"

Nodding, I said, "Yeah, yeah, just thinking. So, why the coverup? Why make it seem that Keith and Tommy died in the firefight at Da Nang?"

Bradwell took a deep drag on his cigarette and blew it out with a sigh. "It was the expedient thing to do." He leaned his elbows on the table and eyed me. "Look, Brandt, this was a big case—really big. We suspected it might reach into the highest levels of both the Vietnamese military and our own. We needed to keep a lid on it or the suspects we knew of would take off, maybe even those we didn't know about. I didn't want word to get around that the Dykstra kid was even there, let alone two of my own agents. So, I got the Marines to play along with my charade." He waved a hand in front of him, fanning away the tobacco smoke or dismissing the impact of his decision, I wasn't sure. "It didn't hurt anyone, right?"

I took a long, angry breath while my teeth gritted, but said nothing.

"Look, Brandt, you've got to understand we were investigating a crime during a very unpopular war this country wanted nothing more to do with," he said. "If word got out about all this black-market profiteering on the taxpayer's dime, Washington would have pulled all of us out of there, toot suite. And that would've been the end of the investigation."

"And the investigation continued?" I asked.

Bradwell leaned back and gave a slight shrug. "Well, ah, yeah. Yeah, it took us longer than it would have with the Dykstra kid's help, but we rolled it up. Quite a feather in my cap, too, let me tell you."

An expensive feathered cap, I thought.

I pulled out the photo of Thomas Danner and laid it on the table. "This man look familiar to you?"

Bradwell glanced at it and shook his head. "No, should he?"

I put the picture of Keith and the others next to Danner's photo. "His name is Thomas Danner," I said, tapping the Danner photograph. "He's in the high-tech export business in San Diego. A few days ago, Rhonda ran into him, and she swore he was Tommy Dykstra." I tapped Tommy's picture. "Said he even had a Marine Corps tattoo in the same place on the same arm as Tommy. And he had a nervous mouth tic, like Tommy did. So, I ask you, does this man look like Tommy Dykstra?"

Bradwell picked up the Danner photo. In a moment, his mouth turned down in an angry frown, and his hands trembled. He let the picture drop onto the table, shaking his head.

"No." He said it in such a way I wondered whether he was trying to convince me or himself. "No. I mean, well, there is a resemblance, yeah. But … a lot of people look like other people." Bradwell smashed out his smoke and lit another. "They say everyone has a—what do they call them? A doppelgänger." He pushed Danner's photo away from him. "Why don't you ask him?"

"I intend to," I said, picking up both photos and slipping them back into my pocket.

Bradwell checked his watch. "Look, like I told you, I've got a noontime tee off." He stood, and I followed suit. "Sorry about your brother, but I can tell you the Dykstra kid is dead. I saw his body with his dog tags."

Dog tags … closed coffin …

"You mean you only ID'd his body from reading his dog tags?" I asked.

"Sure, what d'ya expect?" Bradwell said. "It wasn't only the explosions. There was a fire after that. The whole dive burned down." He led me back into the house, through the wood-paneled living room, to the front door, where he stopped. "So, if you talk to his guy—what's his name again?"

"Thomas Danner," I replied. "And I *will* talk to him."

"Yeah, and when you do, what do you think he'll tell you?" Bradwell's dull gray eyes bore into mine. "What're you going to ask him?"

"If he *is* Tommy Dykstra, I'm going to ask him what *really* happened in that bar," I said, staring back. "And why he's still alive and Keith isn't?"

"What really—" Bradwell's stare became threatening. "Look here, Brandt, I understand how you must feel about your brother, but don't you think you're making a mountain out of a mole hill? I tell you, there is no way this Danner guy is Dykstra—"

"Whether it's a mountain or a molehill, it's mine to climb," I said.

"Yeah, well, just be careful which hills you climb," he said, opening the door. "This one isn't worth dying on."

I stepped through the door and turned back to face him. "Is that a threat?"

"No, just sound advice," he said, and slammed the door.

Chapter 22

I TOOK THE FREEWAY all the way back to San Diego, but I wasn't in a hurry to get home. Something kept scratching at the back of my mind. Why did Bradwell lie to me about his get-away cabin being in Mexico? The little fishing village in the photograph was Puerto Buena in Costa Rica, a fishing village on the northern Caribbean coast of the country, so remote few have ever heard of it. In the Eighties, journalists covering the wars in Nicaragua and El Salvador knew well the log-walled cantina called Te Mana. It was our refuge, somewhere we went to drink ourselves into stupors and, for a while, forget the sights and stink of war.

He also lied about not thinking Thomas Danner and Tommy Dykstra were the same person. That I was damn sure of. The photo of Danner fractured something inside him, something he wanted—needed—to believe for decades, that Tommy Dykstra died in that Saigon bar. But why was *that* so important to him?

And what else did he lie about?

I crossed into the city limits, took the La Jolla exit, and dropped onto La Jolla Village Drive, which led me to the university and its squatting, UFO-like campus library. Again, I scoured through microfiche news stories from over two decades before, searching for any mention of a black-market ring being busted up in Saigon in the early- to mid-1970s.

Without a doubt, there was a black-market problem in Vietnam during the war. No war ever existed without one. But according to contemporary news stories and academic papers published afterward, the illegal sale and purchase of military equipment and supplies during that war surpassed the worldwide black-marketeering seen in WWII. According to a news report from 1966, the United States was "indirectly supplying the enemy with arms and materials thanks to the rampaging black market" in Vietnam.

President Gerry Ford, then a congressman, claimed in a 1966 speech, "The black marketeering carried on by GIs during World War II merely put dollars in their pockets, but the black-market activities in Vietnam are helping the enemy fight us."

That same year alone, the military court-martialed forty-one GIs for black marketeering. Even as Americans pulled out of the war in the early Seventies, the black market in Vietnam continued to grow. Interestingly, despite the communist victory in 1975, Ho Chi Minh City—as the communists renamed Saigon—continued to be the black-market hub of Southeast Asia.

At least Bradwell didn't lie about that. Nonetheless, I found no mention of a major black-market operation broken up in the mid-1970s. Busting something as big as the racket Bradwell described should have generated headlines, not only because of Congress's interest in war-time black marketeering but also because federal agencies make a practice of boasting about their accomplishments. Their funding depends on it.

So, did Bradwell lie about investigating a big black market in 1972? I doubted that. The news stories and government reports from the time confirm the problem existed. Had he lied about breaking up the operation, despite the supposed death of his top informant, Tommy Dykstra? I believed he did. But perhaps he lied to save face rather than admit it was a total cockup that got Tommy and my brother killed. That would mesh with him forcing Keith's commanding officer to lie about how the two died.

Finished with my research, I stood and stretched, then crossed to windows that formed the outer wall of the library. From my second-floor perch, I could look out over the parking lot. I spotted my Mustang and, parked a few slots away, sat a familiar small green sedan. Through the front window, I watched the driver as he read a newspaper, his blue trilby peeking over the top of the pages.

Tygard.

I slipped out of the library through a side entrance and made a wide arc through the parking lot until I stood behind Tygard's car. He was still reading the newspaper, with the driver-side window rolled down. As quietly as possible, I crept toward the open window. I don't know why I did it. Maybe I wanted to show him what it was like to be sur-veilled. Or maybe I wanted to play spy.

"Good afternoon, Mr. Brandt," Tygard said as I reached his left rear fender. He hadn't even looked away from his newspaper.

I sighed and stepped up to his window. "How long did you know?"

"Oh, I saw you watching me from the second-floor win-dow. And also from the time you came around the corner of this … strangely shaped building," he said, folding the newspaper and laying it on the passenger seat. "Is it sup-posed to look like an alien spacecraft?"

"I don't know," I said. "I'm not much into modern ar-chitecture."

"Nor am I." He sighed. "In my academic career, I al-ways preferred halls of ivy. Tell me, how did your meeting with Special Agent Bradwell, retired, go?"

"How did you know I met with Bradwell?" I'd assumed Tygard had followed me all morning, but I didn't think he'd known who I met.

"I'm a spy," he answered. "That's what we do."

"You know Bradwell?"

"I know of him," the Mossad agent replied. "From time to time he has come across our—as you say—radar screen. Was he helpful? Did you learn anything of interest?"

"I learned you were wrong," I answered, leaning my butt on his front fender.

"How so?"

"My brother, Keith, didn't desert, nor was he involved in any black market," I said. "His CO ordered him to go to Saigon with Tommy Dykstra to keep tabs on him."

"Well, that must be a relief to hear," Tygard said. "Anything else?"

"He lies."

"That's not unusual in our trade," the agent said. "For spies and counterspies, lying is part of the job. I suspect the same is true in your profession."

I *did* lie to Bradwell and others about my research into Keith's death. Well, bent the truth a bit. I nodded.

"How did he lie? Please tell me."

"He lied about having a cabin in Mexico," I said. "I saw a photo of him posing in a small fishing village in Costa Rica called Puerto Buena. Reporters used to go there for

R&R when I worked down south. But he said the pic was taken in Mexico."

"Ah! And … what else?"

"I showed him Thomas Danner's photograph and asked him if he thought Danner could be Dykstra. He said 'no.' "

"But …?"

"His physical reaction told me otherwise," I said. "He looked like he was having a stroke."

"Interesting. Anything else?"

"He lied about breaking up a black-market operation in Vietnam," I told him. "Tommy got involved in the operation and got caught. Bradwell's agents wanted to turn him into an informant. He was meeting them in a bar in Saigon to turn over evidence when the bar blew up."

"Killing your brother and his friend."

"And two of Bradwell's agents," I added. "Bradwell claims he later busted the operation, but I can't find news stories or documents showing a major black-market bust occurred in the Seventies. That's what I was doing in the library."

"I see," Tygard said. "And what do you plan for the rest of your day, may I ask?"

I smiled. "Just going home and working on my book. You might as well take the rest of the day off."

The Mossad man gave me a tight smile. "Thank you. I may do that." He started his car. "Oh, and Mr. Brandt?" I stood up and leaned closer to his window. "That is good news about your brother. I hope it helps you rest more easily now."

The window rolled up with an electric whine, and Tygard backed out of the parking slot and drove toward the exit.

Later that night, after Lindbergh Field ended out-bound flights and Jack lay curled asleep on the sofa, I stepped out onto my front porch to enjoy the night sky and the quiet. A flicker of light a few doors down the street grabbed my attention. It came from a small green sedan. As I gazed at the vehicle, the cabin light came on again and, for an instant, I glimpsed Tygard's face smiling at me. Then the light flicked off.

Lies, even the smallest of them, were just part of the job.

Chapter 23

LIFE, SOMEONE ONCE SAID, is what happens when we're busy making other plans. As I told Bradwell, I intended to confront Thomas Danner and find out, once and for all, if he was Tommy Dykstra, and if so, what happened to Keith and did he, TD, kill Rhonda? I would have done so that evening, ambushing him at the bayfront hotel where he stopped for drinks after work—whatever kind of work he actually did. But when I got home, I found two urgent phone messages waiting for me. One came from my publisher, demanding to know why I hadn't sent him the chapter I'd promised to send him two days ago.

The second was from the Los Angeles bureau chief of the newsweekly I freelanced for asking me to cover a science conference in San Diego later in the week. They were planning to profile the featured speaker and wanted me to cover his remarks. The subject didn't interest me, but the income did. As someone also once said, paying bills was the cost of living—probably the same wag who ruminated about life.

I spent the rest of that afternoon and most of the next day finishing and refining the chapter in question before sending it off to my publisher. After that, I spent two days covering the conference and writing up my dispatch before emailing it to my bureau chief. The following morning, Jack had a vet appointment, which meant spending the best part of an hour trying to persuade him to come out of hiding and struggling to get him into the carrier. By mid-afternoon I cleared my desk of any commitments, doctored the scratches Jack left on my arms, and called Jo to ask for another favor.

"Hello?"

I heard murmuring voices in the background and the clink of dishes.

"Hi, it's me."

"I know," she said. "What's up?"

"That NCIS friend of yours," I said. "Could you contact him again and ask him another question about Bradwell?"

"Why don't you ask him yourself?" she replied. "He's right here. We're having drinks."

"I thought you said you were going to have coffee with him," I said. I felt my throat tighten with suspicion.

"It turned into after-work drinks," she said. Then, with her mouth away from the phone, she said, "Rick, it's Peter. He'd like to ask another question about Bradwell."

I glanced at my watch. It seemed early for after-work drinks. A male voice said, "Hello?"

His wasn't a particularly manly voice. Visions of Sean Connery or Roger Moore as James Bond didn't pop into my head. I cleared my throat to loosen its tightness.

"Hi, ah, Rick, is it?"

"Yeah. Peter?"

"That's right," I said. "Jo told me you and Bradwell worked together."

"I had that distinct displeasure, yes," Rick said.

Okay. So, I was beginning to like the guy.

"So, did he ever mention anything about breaking up a major black-market operation during his time in Vietnam?"

Rick didn't answer for a moment. I could almost hear the gears in his head clicking as he searched his memory.

"No, not that I recall," he said. "And he *always* bragged about his time in Nam. Old war stories, you know? Busting up Viet Cong spy rings, drug smugglers, money laundering—that kind of stuff. And girls. Always talking about the girls. Sorry, I guess that's no help."

"No, that's very helpful. Thanks," I told him. "Can I talk to Jo again?"

"Hi," Jo said. "Was that any help?"

"Yeah, it was," I said. "How much longer you going to be?"

"Not much. Rick has to pick up one of his kids in half an hour."

"Oh, good," I said.

"Oh, good?" Jo repeated. "Are we feeling a little—"

"Nothing like that," I said. "I was wondering if you would feed Jack later. I'm going to be home late."

"What's up?"

"I've got to meet a guy for drinks later myself."

"A guy?" Now Jo sounded suspicious.

"Yeah, a guy. Look, if you can't do it, I'll call Cindy and ask her."

"*I'll* feed Jack," Jo said. "And we'll both be waiting up for you, mister."

"Love you, too," I said, and hung up.

The bar was typical for a waterfront hotel. Potted palms and fronds, Jimmy Buffett on the overhead speakers, cocktails with little umbrellas and long straws, and bamboo everywhere—all intended to make the patrons believe they were sipping their chichi drinks on some tropical isle instead of in a hotel built on a manmade island only yards from an international airport in semi-arid Southern California. The young man working the bar was one of those Hollywood-type bartenders who earned large tips by entertaining guests as he juggled bottles while mixing exotic drinks. He seemed disappointed when I ordered scotch and water.

Thomas Danner ambled in around 6 p.m. and sat at the far end of the bar nearest the entrance. His usual spot, I deduced—a perch from which he could view the entire bar and beat a hasty exit if needed. That and the fact the bartender placed his drink in front of that seat before Danner even sat down. I let him settle in and drink his cocktail before I paid off my bar tab and sauntered over to him and sat down.

"Thomas Danner, isn't it?" I asked.

He peered at me with dark, beady eyes. "Do I know you?" he replied, though I sensed he somehow recognized me.

I shook my head. "No, but you knew my brother, Keith Brandt, and his fiancée, Rhonda."

"No," he said, without even wracking his memory. "I'm afraid you're mistaken."

I placed the photo of Keith, Rhonda, and Tommy on the bar in front of him. He squinted at the picture, then at me, and shook his head. "Sorry."

"Come on now," I chided. "Look closer. See, that's Keith, your best friend in the Marines, and that's Rhonda. And that—" I tapped his picture. "That's Tommy Dykstra— a younger you with another name."

"Sorry," he said, shaking his head. "You're mistaking me for someone else. I've never been in the Marines—"

"I know about the Marine Corps anchor and globe tattoo on your arm. My brother had the same tatt. You both got them together."

His hand slipped over his right forearm as if trying to hide the tattoo, even though he wore a long-sleeved shirt and jacket.

"Look again, Tommy," I said, tapping the photo.

He looked and his mouth twitched beneath the cheesy mustache.

"And I know about your nervous tic," I said. "The same tic Tommy Dykstra had."

His hand went to his mouth. He continued staring at the photo, swallowing hard, as if forcing something down. He looked at me and, damn if there weren't tears glistening in his eyes.

"Why are you still alive and my brother isn't?" I asked, keeping my voice low but firm, and staring straight into his watery eyes.

Danner nibbled at his mustache and glanced around the room as if searching for someone to come to his rescue or, perhaps, come to arrest him. He looked at the photo again, sniffed, then he pushed it back to me.

"I can't talk here," he whispered. "I have a boat in the marina. Follow my car there."

He dropped a twenty on the bar, stood, straightened his coat, and walked from to the parking lot as if he had many drinks or, more likely, like he was scared stiff. Feeling pretty damn scared myself, I followed him at a distance, taking my time. After all, I was following a scared animal into his lair, and scared animals are always the most dangerous.

Chapter 24

DANNER WAITED FOR ME at the marina gate, his eyes shifting and probing the dark parking lot. When he saw me, he made a point of scouring the dark over my shoulder for anyone I may have brought along.

"I'm alone," I said.

"Took your time," Danner replied. "What? You get lost?"

"There's only one road to this marina," I said. "I didn't think I had to ride your tail."

Danner glanced around the parking lot again, nodded, and muttered, "Okay." He unlocked the gate, nodded me through, and closed it behind us. As we walked down the gangway with him behind me, my fear quotient shot up as I realized he could blind side me if he wished. But as we reached the dock, he simply brushed past me. "This way," he said.

He led me down the finger pier to his boat, the Suzanne. I pointed out the name and, trying to make conversation, asked, "Old girlfriend?"

Danner grunted but said nothing. We stepped aboard the Suzanne, and he unlocked the cabin door, leading the way below deck. He flipped a switch, and the lights came on. "There's beer in the fridge," he said as he walked through the small galley toward the bow sleeping compartment. "Get us a couple while I change."

I did as told and placed the two bottles on the small dining table. When Danner came out of the forward compartment, he wore jeans and a T-shirt, his Marine Corps tattoo exposed on his right forearm. But it wasn't the tatt that held my attention. It was the .38 revolver he pointed at me.

"Just who the hell are you?" he demanded.

"I'm Peter Brandt, Keith's little brother," I said, not moving anything but my lips.

"Like hell," he said. Danner picked up a TV remote from the kitchenette counter and pressed a button. The little TV/VCR hanging from the bulkhead flashed on, and he used the gun barrel to gesture at it. "Explain this."

The television displayed a video of me entering the cabin, dressed as some kind of boat bum, and snooping around. I scanned the cabin overhead and spotted the video camera sitting inside a glass cabinet where it watched over the interior of the boat.

"One of the nice things about dealing in technology is I get all the latest toys," Danner said. "That camera has a motion sensor and automatically records any movement in here when I'm out. Now, who are you and why'd you break into my boat?"

"I *am* Keith's brother," I said, talking slowly so I could think up a lie. As much experience as I have with lying, I always find it more difficult when someone points a gun at me. "I was trying to find out who you were, if you were Tommy Dykstra like Rhonda claimed. And to find out if you killed her."

"You have some ID?" Danner asked.

I took my wallet from my pocket and showed him my driver's license. He dropped the remote, grabbed the wallet, and flipped through it until he found my press credentials.

"A reporter, huh?"

I shrugged. "It's a living."

He tossed the wallet onto the table. "Reporters always go around breaking into places like that?"

"It's been known to happen."

"You know I can shoot you right now and say it was self-defense," he said. "Say you followed me from the bar and broke in here."

"You won't shoot me," I said. "Not with that pistol."

Danner snickered. "And why not?"

"The problem with revolvers is the person you're pointing them at can look at the cylinder to see if it's loaded," I said. "The cylinder is empty. And …" I gestured toward the TV. "When I was in here before, I saw you don't even have bullets for that gun."

Any sense he had control of the situation vanished. Danner's mouth twitched. His mustache turned down as he looked at the empty cylinder himself. With a look of distaste, he tossed the pistol onto the galley's bench seat.

"I hate guns," he said. He grabbed a beer, twisted it open, and took a lengthy gulp.

I picked up my beer and opened it. "You were a Marine and you hate guns?"

"I hated the Marines," he said.

"Why'd you join up?"

"I didn't have a choice," Danner said. "It was that or go to jail." He plopped onto the bench and chugged some more beer. "That's the story of my life, you know? Always having to choose between two shitty choices. Like that movie with Meryl Streep. What's it called?"

"*Sophie's Choice*?"

"Yeah, that's it. My folks split up when I was a kid. She was a whore, a prostitute, and he was a grifter, a con man. Which one did I want to go with? I went with my old man.

At least I wouldn't have strange men coming to the house day and night.

"He taught me everything he knew about the grift, my old man did," Danner continued, shaking his head. "What a father. Used me in all his cons. When he got too old and lazy or too drunk to do his own cons, he made me pull them off. At eighteen, I finally got caught. The judge told me prison or the Marines." Danner chuckled. "I guess the old fart thought he was doing me a favor. He said the Marines would straighten me out, give me a second chance at life." Danner scoffed. "But you know what? I found out there's just as much grift in the military as in civilian life. You only have to know how to play the game."

"So, you are Tommy Dykstra?" I asked.

Danner leaned across the table at me. "I *was* Tommy Dykstra," he said. "Tommy Dykstra died in that Saigon bar with your brother—my friend, my *only* friend—Keith."

The questions piled up in my brain, each demanding prominence. What happened in the bar that day? How did he survive and not Keith? Why did everyone think he was dead? And, of course, did he kill Rhonda? But I didn't need to choose which one. Danner set the ball rolling.

"I remember meeting you now," he said, tipping the beer bottle in my direction. "You were just a little squirt. Your folks brought you and Rhonda to the amphib to say goodbye to Keith before we shipped out. He introduced me to your parents and you. Called you a 'squirt'."

"Yeah, I recall," I said.

"He wasn't supposed to be there that day, you know," he continued. "I got into some trouble over in Nam. I was going to meet a couple Navy narcs and turn over some info on the black market." Danner shook his head. "See? Again, choosing between two shitty choices, go to prison or turn snitch. I turned snitch. I was supposed to meet them in that bar—alone. But the CO sent Keith with me, I guess, to keep an eye on me."

"I know," I said, and his head jerked up. "I spoke with two of your platoon mates and your platoon leader."

Danner snorted. "You really are a reporter, aren't you?"

I nodded. "Tell me what happened."

"Nothing," Danner said. "We drank some beers. I hoped Keith would get bored and take off on his own, and finally he did. When he left, I nodded at the agents and gestured I needed to piss. The bar only had a one-holer, and it was occupied. I couldn't hold it, so I stepped out into the alley and peed like a racehorse. I was buttoning my pants up when the first bomb went off. It threw me against the opposite building. Before I could get up, another bomb went off. By the time I ran into the bar, the whole place was burning. I don't know shit about bombs, but I smelled something like gasoline or some other chemical—"

"You mean like an accelerant?" I asked.

"Yeah, like that," he agreed. "I was shocked when I saw Keith's body on the floor 'cause I thought he'd left—"

"He ran back in to get you," I said.

Danner looked at me, his eyes tearing again, and nodded. "Yeah, figured that's what happened, too." He took a gulp of beer and swallowed hard. "Anyway, I couldn't do anything for him. He was dead already, and his body burning."

"Why did you run and disappear like you did?" I asked.

"I got scared," Danner said. "That wasn't some VC throwing a couple of grenades into a bar. That was the black-market gang. I needed to get out of there, get away and hide. I saw a dead grunt near the door. Probably the guy in the head came out just as the bombs went off. His body was burning, too. So, I took off my dog tags and swapped them for the dead guy's tags."

Bradwell's assurance came back to me. *"I can tell you the Dykstra kid is dead. I saw his body with his dog tags."*

Dog tags ... closed coffin ...

I shook myself out of my own thoughts and asked, "Then what?"

"Then I ran for my life," Danner said. "And I've been running ever since."

Chapter 25

"BUT WHY RUN?" I repeated. "Why not go back to the NIS? They'd protect you."

Danner laughed. "Like hell!" he said and laughed again. "Who the hell do you think blew the fucking bar up? The head of the NIS office there! That's who I was going to finger to those two agents of his. He was part of the black-market ring."

"Nelson Bradwell?"

"Yeah," Danner said. "On one of my drop-offs, I spotted him leaving the warehouse where they kept the goods. Didn't know who the hell he was, but when his agents dragged me into their offices a couple of weeks later, I saw him there. That's when I knew I could make a deal. But when the bar blew up, I knew Bradwell had to be involved somehow, so I took off."

"And then?"

"I had some money, and I knew my way around the black market, so I bought myself some ID saying I was an Air Force airman. And the crews of those cargo planes going in and out of the country—" He snorted. "Hell, some of them will smuggle anything or anyone for a price. So, I ended up in Thailand with a new name."

"But you stayed involved with the black market," I said. "Why?"

Danner looked at me sharply. "No," he hissed, "I'm a legit businessman."

"After Tommy Dykstra, you were Tobias Denton," I replied. "Now you're Thomas Danner. How legit is that?"

Danner stared at me for a long while, then snorted and shook his head. "You *are* some hot-shot reporter, aren't you?" He drank more beer and pointed the bottle at me again. "Keith would've been proud of you."

"No," I said. "He'd still call me shrimp."

"I like to say I'm in import-export," Danner said.

"High-tech smuggling, you mean."

He shrugged. "I prefer smuggler to black marketeer," he said.

"That's how you ran into Rhonda," I told him, "making a deal to sneak her company's tech somewhere where it shouldn't go, right?"

"I have clients who the government sometimes frowns on," Danner said. "I help facilitate their acquisition of certain technologies that otherwise would not be available to them."

"Sounds like you've practiced that line a lot," I said.

Danner leaned back and laughed. "Boy, have I. Sometimes I can repeat it in a fairly good Limey accent, too." He emptied his beer and pulled another from the refrigerator. "You want another?" I shook my head. He opened the bottle and sat back down. "And, let me tell you, that company of Rhonda's isn't exactly on the up and up itself." He took a deep gulp, looking at me queerly. "Wait—" he said. "How do you know Bradwell?"

Things started clicking into place. Bradwell's reaction to Danner's photo. His lying about breaking up the black market. The cover story about Keith and TD dying in the Da Nang attack. Bradwell wanted both TD *and* his agents dead—TD because he recognized him as one of the black marketeers, and the agents because they suspected Bradwell.

I couldn't tell Danner yet that I'd spoken with Bradwell; I still needed more information from him. Instead, I said, "Your platoon leader told me the NIS Saigon station chief was the guy who wanted you and Keith listed as KIA. I dug around and learned his name."

He thought about that awhile, nodded, and said, "Oh, right, you're a reporter."

I nodded. "Now tell me about Rhonda."

Danner shrugged, shaking his head. "What about her?"

"Why did you murder her?"

Danner's fist slammed the table. *"I did not murder her!"* He glared at me for at least a full minute, his chest heaving, then slumped back into the bench seat and rubbed his eyes. "I didn't *murder* her. I *loved* her. Always had a thing for her."

"You're saying you *didn't* kill Rhonda?" I asked.

Tears streamed down from his clenched eyes as he ran his hands through his hair. First, he shook his head, then he nodded. "I did," he murmured. "I killed her. But I didn't *murder* her. I would never *murder* Rhonda. It—it was an accident." His sodden red eyes were pleading. "There's a difference, isn't there?"

I looked down and saw my own hands clenching the edge of the table, the knuckles a bloodless white. Consciously, I relaxed my hands and gave them a little shake to get the blood back into them. With my voice tight, I said, "Tell me what happened."

"I—I stopped in the hotel bar like I do most nights," he explained. "I didn't know she was staying there. You know, when I met with her and the others, I didn't recognize her at first—not until I heard her name. And I didn't think she recognized me … you know, it's been a long time. But I didn't want to take any chances, and as soon as I saw her in the bar, I left. But she must've seen me 'cause as I was getting into my car, I heard her call out, 'TD!' That's what they used to call me, you know? And after all these goddamn years, I instinctively turned around. That's when she knew for sure I was Tommy Dykstra."

"Did you talk to her?" I asked.

"Hell, no," Danner said. "I got in my car and drove off like a banshee. But she followed me again. I struggled to get that damn marina gate open when she caught up with me. She said, 'TD, I know it's you. I know it's you, TD. Where's Keith?' She was drunk, slurring her words. I got the gate open and ran down the plank to the boat. Thought I'd gotten away from her, but she must've pushed through the gate before the damn thing locked. I got on the boat and thought about casting off and going offshore for a couple of days. Maybe she'd sober up, forget about me. But then the boat heeled over, and she was yelling, 'TD! TD! TD!'"

Danner swallowed more beer and wiped his mouth with his arm. "I finally got her to quiet down and invited her to come below. I thought I could reason with her, convince her I wasn't TD, that maybe I just looked like him. But she went ballistic again and started yelling, 'Where's Keith? Where's Keith? You're alive. Keith must be alive.' She kept getting louder. I thought she'd wake the whole damn marina, so I tried to muffle her and—" His head dropped into his hands, and he sobbed. "God help me, I somehow smothered her or choked her. The next thing I knew, she was dead in my arms."

Danner crossed his arms on the table and rested his head, his shoulders heaving, sobbing. I finished my beer in a couple of gulps and watched him, uncertain whether I should pity him or kill him. Was he really a tortured soul, or just a good con man? After a few minutes, I said. "So, you dumped her in the bay so it looked like she drowned?"

"I've got a little motor skiff tied up on the outboard side," Danner continued, his voice muffled in his arms. "I slipped her into the boat and motored out into the bay and put her over the side. Then I came back and collected her shoes and purse, drove them down the island a bit in her rental car, and put them on the rocks so it'd look like she drowned herself. I left the rental there and walked back to the boat." Lifting his head, he peered at me with sunken eyes. "I—I didn't know what else to do."

He lowered his head again, and mumbled, "I'm sorry, Rhonda. I'm so sorry."

Chapter 26

AFTER A WHILE, HE asked, "Wha— what are you going to do? Turn me in?"

I thought about it for a while. "I promised someone I wouldn't monkey in his investigation. Lieutenant McCarty—you've met him. I think you should turn yourself in and explain what happened with Rhonda. You might get away with manslaughter instead of murder."

His head shot up, his eyes widening. "Are you crazy? With my background? No way!"

"I don't think you have a choice," I told him. "Bradwell knows about you. He knows you're alive and living here as Thomas Danner."

Danner stared at me in disbelief as he sank deeper into the bench seat, his face paling. "No. No," he said, shaking his head. "No, how can that be? How could he know?"

"I'm afraid that's my fault," I explained. "I talked to Bradwell a few days ago, trying to find out what happened the day Keith died, and showed him the photo from your brochure. He denied it, but I know he recognized you."

With an animalistic groan, Danner lurched out of his seat and paced the cabin, hands tearing at his hair. "How could you? How—how could you do that?"

"I didn't know he was the bad guy," I said lamely.

"Do you understand what this means? I've got to get out of here! I've got to start all over again!"

"I don't think that's an option, TD," I said. Danner turned and glared at me, waiting for me to continue. "Now that he knows you're still alive, Bradwell will hunt you down wherever you go. He's a retired fed. He's still got connections. Forget the black market in Nam—Bradwell murdered Keith and two NIS agents. There's no statute of limitations on murder. And you're the only one who can link him to those murders."

"And that's why I have to run again!" Danner cried.

"No, that's why you *can't* run," I argued. "He'll find you. Look, Customs have their eye on you, too. That's how I know about your other alias, Tobias Denton." I left out that the Israeli Mossad had an interest in him, too. "If they know where you are, Bradwell will know. You drop the dime on Bradwell, he goes to prison. You plea deal on Rhonda's death, and you live. Maybe they'll put you in the Witness

Protection Program, give you a new identity—an identity that will hold water. *That's* why you have to turn yourself in."

Danner stopped pacing and stared at the ceiling. "So, here I am again," he said, "another Sophie's Choice. Snitch and go to prison or let Bradwell kill me. Just like the baseball guy said, 'Déjà vu all over again.'"

He let out a groan of frustration as he ran his hands over his face, then threw himself into a chair and sat in silence. Finally, he looked at me and said, "The Marines'll be after me for desertion, you know."

"Maybe … probably." I shrugged. "But Bradwell murdered two federal agents, two NIS agents. That's makes it a federal crime, with NCIS or the FBI leading the investigation. You can plea deal that, too."

Danner rolled his eyes and made a sardonic chuckle. "That's what got me in this mess in the first place."

"Sorry, but those are the only options I see," I told him.

Biting his lower lip, Danner started nodding. "Damned if I do, damned if I don't," he said. "Story of my life." I nodded in agreement. "All right. Who do I turn myself in to?"

"Mike McCarty," I said. "He's leading the Rhonda investigation and can keep you safe until everything else gets settled. I know a guy in NCIS who'd love to hear your story about Bradwell. You can talk to him next."

Danner nodded again. "When?"

"Now." I stood and checked my watch. "I'll call Mike and drive you to the cop shop. He can meet us there."

Again nodding, he stood and said, "Let me get a coat."

He went into the forward compartment and came back wearing a leather jacket. Without another word, we left the cabin and climbed onto the dock. I took out my cell phone and started looking through the directory for Mike's mobile number when the phone on the Suzanne started ringing.

"Let me get that," Danner said, jumping onto the boat.

As I waited, I called McCarty. His voice mail answered. "Mike, Peter Brandt," I began. "I'm here with—"

I have no clear memory of what happened next. A bright flash like lightning. A fist the size of King Kong's slammed into me, hurling me into the water between two docked yachts. An incredible roar screamed in my ears. Water enveloped me. Everything blurred. Sound muffled. What seemed a century or two later, I went up instead of down, or perhaps it was the other way around. A sharp tug, and I'm lifted from the water and land back on the dock, gasping for breath, my eyes burning from the oily salt water.

Seconds became minutes, minutes became an eternity— I'm not sure. The dock reverberated with pounding footsteps. A fire crackled. Smoke made the air acrid. And the stench of burnt meat. Voices hovered around and above me, murmurs muffled by the ringing in my ears. One sounded familiar, saying something about calling an ambulance. Days later, or maybe only minutes, the high-pitched scream of sirens. Voices yelling. I'm lifted again and laid on something firm, but not as hard as the dock. Bouncing, pulled one way, then the other. Doors slamming down toward my feet, followed only by blackness.

There are dreams, and then there are dreams. Dreams we wish and long for, and dreams we want to run away from. This was one of the latter.

I'm walking down a street crammed with bars and night clubs and restaurants, all with signs written in some Asian language. Like China Town in Los Angeles, but the signs are not in Chinese. Words written in a Roman-like alphabet, but the words are all foreign to me, full of accent and pronunciation marks in strange places. Nearly everyone on the street is Asian. Old women in conical hats. Young men in military uniforms. Young, beautiful women in tight-fitting, full-length dresses split up the side. Motor scooters and tricycle-like rickshaws crowd the street.

Ahead of me, I see a young Marine walk out of a bar. I catch only a brief glimpse of his face, but I recognize him. Keith. I yell for him, but my voice doesn't seem to carry. Trying to wave at him, my arms feel heavy and immobile. I run, but it feels like wading through molasses. But I need to reach him, need to tell him, need to warn him.

The blast sends me reeling backwards. As I clamber to my feet, I see Keith through the smoke stagger to his feet. I yell at him again. I scream at him. But he doesn't hear. In slow motion, I watch as he races back into the bar. The second blast again sends me reeling, falling, flailing into a dark void. An old man peers down at me. A westerner, with thick white hair and dead blue eyes. I hear my voice screaming, "Nooooo!"

I felt hands on my shoulders, gentle, caring, and I opened my eyes to find Jo hovering over me, comforting me. We were in a hospital room. Machines beeped an electronic beat. The room smelled of alcohol and sanitizers. I looked at Jo again and she smiled.

"Welcome back to the world, mister," she said.

Chapter 27

I REMAINED CONSCIOUS FOR only a few minutes, long enough for Jo to explain that Danner's boat exploded; that Danner was dead; that I nearly drowned; that the doctors kept me in a medically induced coma for two days to prevent my brain from swelling and were now allowing me to come out of it. She told me all of that, and then I slipped back into the darkness.

When I woke the next morning, I found Jo still there. Mike McCarty and Dick Sanders were there, too. My head throbbed and my stomach churned. The overhead lights seemed unnecessarily bright. Jo helped me drink some water. A nurse came with a breakfast tray, but all I could stomach was some black coffee.

"Well, if you're not going to eat this—" Jo slapped Sanders' hand as he reached for a piece of toast.

"You feel up to talking, Pete?" Mike asked.

I sipped some more coffee and nodded gently—very gently.

"What happened on the boat?" he asked.

"You mean what put me in the hospital?" I shook my head and regretted it. "I don't know. Don't you?"

"We know Danner's boat blew up," Sanders said gruffly, still eyeing the toast. "We've a pretty good guess it was a bomb. We don't know why. Do you?"

Mike looked sideways at Sanders, his brow furrowed. "Let's start at the beginning, Pete," he said. "What were you doing with Danner on his boat? You told me you wouldn't interfere with my murder investigation."

"I just wanted to talk to him," I said. "I wanted to find out if he was TD—Keith's friend, Tommy Dykstra—and what happened to Keith."

"And?" Mike coaxed.

"He is—was TD. He escaped the bomb that killed Keith and, yes, he killed Rhonda," I said. "Killing Rhonda was an accident. She was drunk and hysterical, demanding he tell her about Keith. She believed if TD was alive, Keith should be alive, too. Danner tried to quiet her and accidentally choked her. He didn't mean to kill her."

"And you believed him?" snorted Sanders.

"He was going to turn himself in," I explained. "To you, Mike. We were heading to the station." I squeezed my eyes shut, forcing my memory to cooperate. "We just left the boat … his phone started ringing. He went back to answer it … I started to call you … voicemail … I got your voicemail. That's all I remember."

"That's when the boat exploded," Mike said. "The voicemail picked up the sound of the blast. According to witnesses, you were blown into the water. Some bystander pulled you out, probably saved your life."

"Who?"

Mike shrugged. "Don't know. He left before the fire department and the harbor police arrived."

"And TD—Danner?" I asked.

"Wasn't much of him left," Mike said.

Another closed coffin burial for Tommy Dykstra.

"Why would he be so willing to turn himself in?" Sanders asked. "Doesn't make sense to me."

"There's something else." I closed my eyes again, coalescing my memories. I saw the man from my dream again and his dead blue eyes. "Bradwell," I said. "He believed Nelson Bradwell would come after him."

"Who's Nelson Bradwell?" McCarty asked.

"Retired NCIS," I told them. "NIS station head in Saigon when my brother got killed. Bradwell killed him. He meant to kill TD and two of his agents. TD found out Bradwell was tied up with the local black market and was meeting the agents to give them information. Bradwell succeeded in killing the agents—*and my brother*—but TD escaped and went into hiding."

I turned to Sanders. "You and Tygard were right," I said. "TD was both Tobias Denton and Danner."

McCarty turned to Sanders. "Who's Denton? Who's this Tygard? One of your agents?"

Sanders shrugged Mike's questions away and pointed to his head. "Don't listen to him. He's had his brains scrambled."

Mike eyed the Customs man with suspicion before turning his attention back to me.

"Why was Danner still so afraid of this Bradwell?" he asked. "Is he still alive?"

"Lives in Orange County," I said. "I drove up and talked to him a few days ago about what happened to my brother. He lied about the details. And he thought TD was dead until I showed him Danner's photograph. He recognized Danner as TD. Nearly had a stroke."

"Wait," McCarty said, "are you saying Bradwell blew up the boat?"

"Before he joined NIS, Bradwell worked as a bomb tech for the Orange County Sheriff," I said. "You have to know how to make bombs to disable them. Bradwell planted the bombs that killed Keith and his two agents. Once he realized TD was still alive—thanks to me—he'd have no problem finding out where TD lived. He was an ex-fed, and the feds knew about Danner and his boat."

I looked at Sanders, and Mike followed my stare. "You were investigating Danner, too?"

Sanders, looking guilty, shrugged, and nodded. "Tech smuggling. A Customs case."

"That's how Sanders knew when you started looking at Danner in Rhonda's murder." Sanders gave me another withering look. I ignored him and turned to Mike. "That doesn't matter now. What matters is arresting Bradwell. You need to get the local OC cops to arrest him."

Mike shook his head. "Can't do that just on your suspicion. I need probable cause."

Something else tried to claw its way to the surface of my memory. Closing my eyes, I had a flash of me entering the Suzanne's cabin—that is, watching myself entering.

Watching myself.

"A camera," I said. As I did, I glimpsed Sanders turn away, a look of guilt on his face. "Danner had some kind of automatic video camera set up in his boat. It recorded everyone who entered the boat. If Bradwell entered the boat to plant a bomb, he should be on the video."

"Which is at the bottom of the marina right now," Mike said. "If the blast didn't get it, then the fire did. The fire inspector said some type of accelerant was used as well as an explosive. And if the fire didn't get it—well, like I said, it's at the bottom of the marina."

"Accelerant!" I exclaimed, and lightning shattered my head. "Accelerant," I said softer. "Danner said Bradwell used an accelerant to blow up the bar in Saigon. Burnt it down and everyone inside—including Keith."

Mike scribbled something in a notebook, then put it away. "I'll check it out. If the fire inspector can figure out what kind of accelerant the bomber used, we might be able to connect it with this Bradwell guy. And I'll have our dive team look for that camera. Probably useless, but you never can tell."

As Mike left, I glared at Sanders. "What?" he said.

"You knew about the camera?"

He wagged his head and shrugged. "Well, yeah. Yeah. Tygard noticed it in one of the photos you took inside Danner's boat. A little red light glowed on the front of the camera, showing it was recording."

"And you didn't let Peter know?" demanded Jo.

Sanders looked at the floor and toed the tile with his shoe. "We didn't want to make him nervous," he said.

I leaned back on the pillow, closing my eyes. The world looked so much better that way. When I opened them again, I asked, "Where is Tygard? Tweedle Dee forgot to bring Tweedle Dumb?"

"Spies don't make hospital visits," Sanders said.

"You know that bomb went off as Danner answered the phone," I said. "Didn't the Mossad use that technique when they went after those Munich Olympic terrorists? Maybe that's why Tygard's not here?"

"I read the Mossad stopped using that type of bomb after they killed an innocent bystander," Jo said.

"Tygard's old," I replied. "And you know what they said about old dogs and tricks."

Sanders's head shook with obvious disgust. "You're a fucking moron sometimes, Brandt," he groused. "Who the hell do you think dragged you out of the drink?"

"Tygard?"

He nodded derisively. "Tygard was tailing you, remember?"

"Yes." I nodded, again regretting it.

"I told you we thought you might step into some shit you couldn't get yourself out of. You not only stepped in it, you fell into it face first. And Tygard pulled you out."

"He saved Peter's life," Jo said.

"And not for the first time, I understand," Sanders said. "For some reason I can't understand, I think the old guy likes you."

Chapter 28

THE DOCTORS RELEASED ME the next morning. Hospital rules insisted I be pushed to the entrance in a wheelchair. I protested, insisting I could walk, but a bear of a nurse with the personality of Bigfoot put her big foot down.

"This is fun," Jo said as she pushed me through the corridors with the zeal of a Mario Andretti at a Formula 1 race. "It's good practice."

"Practice for what?"

"For when you get old and decrepit," she replied, "and I have to wheel you around to all your doctor's appointments. You are older than me, remember?"

"Not that much older," I complained.

"Old enough," she said.

"What makes you think we'll be together then?" I asked.

"I told you, we've both put too much into this relationship," Jo replied.

We took an elevator to the ground floor. Just as the doors opened, we ran into Mike McCarty.

"I was coming to see you," he said. He paused and looked me over, turned to Jo and asked, "Is he so bad off, he needs a wheelchair?"

"No, I'm not bad off at all," I grumped. "Hospital rules." I jumped out of the chair and made for the exit. "What's up? You find out anything about Bradwell yet? You find that camera?"

Mike nodded, and we followed Jo to where she parked her car. "Only pieces," he said, "and those were burned or waterlogged." He consulted a notebook he drew from his pocket. "The fire marshal's report came back on the explosive used in the bomb. An ANFO bomb with a radio detonator."

"Ammonium nitrate and fuel oil?" Jo said.

"That's right. A Timothy McVeigh Special," Mike said, referring to the right-wing nutcase who blew up the federal building in Oklahoma City. "In addition to the ANFO, they found toluene residue, probably used as an accelerant to make sure the boat burned. Toluene has a low flash point and has a benzene-like odor." He looked up at me. "You said Danner told you he noticed a chemical smell in the

Saigon bombing?" I nodded. "Well, that might have been toluene, too."

"Where would Bradwell get toluene?" I asked.

"It's used in all kinds of solvents and resins," Mike said. "You can buy it by the gallon at hardware stores. So, of course, we canvased hardware stores in Orange County and guess what? A certain Mr. Nelson Bradwell bought a gallon can of toluene one week ago. Said he was doing some home improvements. And, he also bought a bag of chemical fertilizer."

"That's ammonium nitrate," Jo said.

Mike nodded.

"Seven days ago? That would be right after I talked to him," I said. "That would link Bradwell to the bomb in Danner's boat. Can you get a search warrant?"

"Two of my guys are driving up there right now to serve it with the local PD," Mike said. He put his notebook away and scratched his nose while thinking. "Kind of careless though, isn't it? I mean, for a law enforcement pro to leave such a trail."

"He was in a hurry," I said. "Bradwell needed Danner dead and fast. TD could finger him for Keith's murder *and* the murder of his own agents. There's no statute of limitations on murder."

"Mike nodded, then shrugged. "Anyway, I'll let you know when I hear from my guys."

"Call my home number, Mike," I yelled out as he left the parking lot. "My cell's in the bay."

McCarty waved his acknowledgement.

☼

Jack welcomed me home by circling my legs twice and leading me into the kitchen to refill his kibble bowl. After a few mouthfuls, he returned to the living room and curled up on Jo's lap. So much for missing me.

Too early in the morning for a drink, so I made some coffee, poured two cups, and took them out to the front room. I gave one to Jo and took the other to my desk, where I powered up the computer to check my email.

"Thanks for taking care of Jack, Jo," I said as the machine chirped to life. "And thanks for being there when I woke up."

Jo took a few sips of her coffee and set the cup down. She eased Jack off her lap and laid him on the couch, stood, and walked the short distance to my desk. A pleasant smile graced her lips. I expected her to kiss me. Instead, she slapped me across the head.

"What were you thinking?" she demanded.

"Watch it," I complained, covering my head. "I have a brain injury, remember?"

"Oh, don't worry about that," she hissed. Her eyes had turned her famous *Cold as Ice Rice* blue. "You don't have a brain to injure. First, you break into the man's boat, then you go there to talk to him?"

"I explained why I—"

"You damn near got yourself killed, Peter," Jo yelled. "You could've been in that boat with Danner when the bomb went off. Really, what the hell were you thinking? What?"

Jack leapt off the couch and skulked into the bedroom. I felt like following him and wondered if there was enough room under the bed for both of us.

"I told you—I told you before, we've got too much involved in this relationship," Jo said. "I don't want to lose you again."

"Again?" I asked. "You never lost me, Jo. I lost you—"

"I lost *you* to Robin," she said. "To her memory—to your memory of a broken marriage. That's why you lost me."

"But—"

She hushed me with a sharp wave of her hand. "I know—I know." She paced the small living room. "Then the table turned, and it was my memories of Frank and what he did. But we've been good since then. It hasn't been a long time, but we've been good. And I don't want *that* to end because you got careless."

Standing, I took her in my arms. "I'm sorry," I said. "I shouldn't have gone with him to the boat. That was stupid."

Jo slapped me gently on the shoulder. "Damn right it was." She wiped a tear from under her eye. "Oh, Christ, look at me. Now I have to redo my makeup."

As she walked toward the bedroom and its attached bathroom, I said, "Check under the bed, would you? Let Jack know the coast is clear."

I didn't know at the time that nothing was clear at all.

Chapter 29

AFTER JO LEFT FOR her office, I rummaged through my email. The new chapter pleased my book editor. My science conference coverage made my bureau chief happy. An email from the city college where I taught journalism asked if I could sub for another instructor who was ill. I replied I had had an "accident" myself and begged off.

By noon I hadn't heard from Mike McCarty about the search of Bradwell's home and I started feeling edgy. I thought about taking a run, but my head rejected the idea. For that matter, so did my body—I ached everywhere. Instead, I walked down to the beach and strolled along the esplanade. It was a pleasant day, mildly warm, the sky nearly cloudless. Seagulls squawked as they soared among the breezes. The surf was up, and boarders were taking advantage of it. Sunbathers lounged across the sand, bodies glistening with suntan oil.

I stopped at a beachfront coffee shop and ate a scone washed down with black coffee while I tried to focus on the scenery and not think about the man who killed my brother. It didn't work. I felt even more on edge as the minutes wore on. I reached for my cell phone, then remembered I'd lost it to Davy Jones' Locker.

Finishing my coffee, I strode back to my bungalow. While still in my medically induced coma, Jo had arranged to have my Mustang towed back to the house, where it sat in the driveway. I have to admit, Jo was the most organized person I knew. She thought of everything. I got in and drove over the hill to the Midway District and to the shop where I bought my cell phone.

The kid who waited on me had a long, acne-scarred face and gel-stiffened, spiky black hair, and blood-shot eyes magnified by thick lenses set in horn rims. I told him I needed a new phone.

"Certainly," he said. "May I have your old one?"

"No," I said.

He stared at me. "You're not trading it in?" he asked.

"I lost it," I told him.

"Oh, I see. You misplaced it," he said.

"No, I know exactly where it is."

He peered at me again. "You lost it, but you know exactly where it is?" I nodded. "And where would that be?"

"San Diego Bay."

The kid nodded. "Ah, I see." He made a little clucking sound. "You'd be amazed how often that happens. People drop them from boats all the time."

"No, I went swimming with it," I said.

"In the harbor?" He looked aghast.

"It wasn't my idea," I told him.

Apparently, the kid thought it better not to ask any more questions and set me up with a new phone. I went out to my car and started to call McCarty, but realized there were no contacts in the phone yet, and I couldn't remember Mike's number. With a curse, I drove back to the bungalow.

Jack sat in the window waiting for me. I could hear him howling as I approached the door. Once inside, he trotted into the kitchen, and I followed. "Your kibble bowl is still full, Jack," I told him. "What are you howling about?"

He led me into the bathroom and sat next to his litter box, looked at it, then looked at me. He complained with a loud meow. I found the scoop and started cleaning it. "You know, Jack, heroes in novels never have to clean their cat's litter boxes," I told him. "Why is that?"

As soon as I finished, the landline rang. As I turned to answer the phone, Jack jumped into the box and started digging.

I answered the phone. Mike McCarty, and he didn't sound overjoyed.

"Hey, Pete," he said without enthusiasm.

"Bad news?" I asked. "Your people served the warrant, didn't they?"

"Yeah, and they found the toluene and chemical fertilizer," Mike said. "They also found parts of a cell phone that could've been used to make the radio-controlled detonator."

Good news, but not delivered as such. My grip on the handset tightened. "But what?"

"Bradwell's gone," he said. "His housekeeper said he packed a couple of suitcases and said he wouldn't be back for a while."

"She have any idea where he went or how long he'd be gone?"

"What do you think?" Mike said.

"He's on the run," I said, stating the obvious. "What now?"

"I've already put out a BOLO," he said, cop-talk for Be On the Lookout. "We got his car's description and license plate from the DMV. His picture, too. Nothing so far, but it's early." He paused, then said, "Oh, the local NCIS chief called wanting to be briefed in."

"Guy named Rick?"

"Yeah, friend of yours?"

"No," I said. "Friend of Jo's. Military cops, you know? Rick worked under Bradwell when he was agent in charge here—and he's not too fond of the SOB. He have any ideas?"

"No, but he became interested when I told him Bradwell might be responsible for the death of two Navy agents—oh, and your brother, of course. Said he would look up the old case file."

"Well, thanks for calling, Mike," I said. "Let me know if you hear anything."

"The minute I do," Mike assured me.

I thanked him again and ended the call by calling him Moondoggie, but it gave me no pleasure. My heart wasn't in it.

After hanging up, I called Jo and told her what McCarty said. In turn, she called her friend Rick to see what he knew. Rick said he was still trying to find the quarter-of-a-century-old case file on the two dead NIS agents in Saigon. I called Dick Sanders, but he'd already heard about Bradwell. It wasn't a Customs case, he said, but he asked Immigration to notify him if Bradwell left the country.

I fixed myself a strong scotch and water, grabbed a cigarette from my nightmare stash in the nightstand, and stood on the porch feeling tired, angry, defeated, and powerless.

It's all bullshit, you know. This crap about seeking revenge for the death of a loved one. What did Sam Spade say in *The Maltese Falcon*? "When a man's partner is killed, he's supposed to do something about it. It doesn't make any difference what you thought of him. He was your partner, and you're supposed to do something about it." Why? What difference did it make? Did revenge bring his dead partner back?

Vengeance is mine ... saith the Lord.

What good did revenging his father's murder do Hamlet? After to-being and not-to-being across the stage for three acts and leaving behind a trail of bodies, he finally metes out his revenge only to be repaid with a poison-tipped foil. Shakespeare took some thirty thousand words to say what Vietnam veterans have been saying for twenty-five years in just four: Payback is a motherfuck.

Is it really only about payback?

Years ago, I sought revenge for the murder of my ex-wife, Robin Anderson, when I learned the local cops weren't doing anything about it. Not for any Sam Spade principle, or Biblical judgment, or payback, but because I felt I let her down; I hadn't been there to protect her. Because of my own insecurities, I pushed her away. The marriage failed, and I went off to my own personal exile from which I never completely returned. And when I finally got my revenge, five more people were in their graves and Robin was still dead.

Yeah, it's all bullshit.

So, why was I standing on the porch, a death-grip on my drink and a burnt-down cigarette cooking my fingers? Because I *wanted* revenge. I wanted Bradwell to pay for killing my brother. I wanted revenge for what Keith's death did to my parents—to me, too. And to Rhonda—beautiful, happy, lively Rhonda who ended up dying a lonely, middle-aged lush working for a corrupt tech firm.

Don't you think you're making a mountain out of a mole hill? That's what Bradwell asked me. *A mountain or a mole-hill, it's mine to climb.* That's what I told him. *Yeah, well, just be careful which hills you climb. This one isn't worth dying on.*

Maybe it wasn't.

Then again, maybe it was.

Chapter 30

THAT EVENING, I STILL smoldered about it. Jo came by with takeout Chinese and a bottle of wine. We ate in silence; she knew I didn't feel like talking and I was smart enough to know she did. Afterward, we sat on the couch, Jack snug on her lap, and watched the news. The big story of the day was the death of Britain's Princess Diana, former wife of heir-to-the-crown Prince Charles, in a car crash in Paris. Already the tabloids were hinting at something sinister behind her death.

Jack suddenly leapt from Jo's lap, landing on the floor with his back arched and fur bristling. He let out a growl and a hiss. Then we heard footsteps on the stoop and a knock on the door.

"Calm down, Jack," I said as I opened the door.

Dick Sanders and Tygard stood on the porch, and by their looks, I knew they weren't delivering good news.

"Hey, Brandt," Sanders said. "I—um." He glanced at Tygard. "That is, we have some news on Bradwell and thought we'd best deliver it in person."

Opening the door further, I beckoned them in with a nod. Jack hissed again, then another growl.

"I see you still have that wildcat," Tygard said, eyeing Jack with suspicion.

"Stand down, Jack," I said. "They're friends." I shrugged. "Well, acquaintances anyway."

"I'd rather stay out here, if you don't mind," Tygard said.

"Here, I'll put him in the bedroom," Jo said, picking Jack up.

When she returned, Sanders and Tygard came inside. Jack howled from the bedroom and scratched at the door as if trying to dig his way out of hell.

"That's a very aggressive cat you have, Mr. Brandt," Tygard said, his eyes flitting toward the bedroom door.

"Jack?" Jo said, dismissing the notion. "He's a regular pussycat."

"Okay," I said. "So, what's the news and how bad is it?"

"San Diego PD found Bradwell's car abandoned in San Ysidro near the border," Sanders said.

"Abandoned?" I asked. "Meaning?"

"He appears to have walked across the border," Sanders continued. "Figured he didn't want to fly out of Lindbergh Field, so I had Mexican customs check the passenger lists at Rodriguez International in Tijuana. He flew out this afternoon on a flight to Mexico City. I notified your friend McCarty, and he asked the local police to catch him at the airport, but they were too late. He'd already arrived and left the airport. McCarty's working the phones with Mexico City PD and Interpol, trying to get them to set up a dragnet around the city, so I told him I'd let you know what was happening."

I stared at them for a long time without saying a word, all thoughts obscured by a seething anger. Finally, I took a deep breath and relaxed.

"I need a drink," I said, turning and heading into the kitchen. "You want one?" They both abstained, so I poured a single scotch for myself. When I returned, I said, "They won't find him in Mexico."

Both Sanders and Tygard raised their eyebrows.

"That's just a waypoint to throw everyone off," I added.

"How so, may I ask, Mr. Brandt?" Tygard asked.

"In his house, I saw two photographs of him," I explained. "One of him holding up a marlin he'd caught, another of him at a mountain cabin with a young girl—a very young girl. I guess he caught her, too. When I asked, he claimed the photos were taken in a small Mexican village that gringos never heard of. He called it his own secret hideaway or something like that."

"All right, so he's got a fucking hideaway in Mexico," Sander said. "We'll find it."

"Not in Mexico, you won't," I said. "He lied. I recognized the village in the photo. It's a small town on the northeast coast of Costa Rica called Puerto Buena, up next to the Nicaraguan border. So remote, you can only get there by air or boat, and the only people doing that are hardcore surfers and sports fishermen. When I worked out of Salvador and Nicaragua, some of my journo friends and I'd go there for R&R to avoid the tourists. We'd hang out in this little cantina called Te Mana. In the photo of Bradwell and his catch—that is, the marlin—I saw Te Mana in the background."

"How can you be sure he is headed there, Mr. Brandt?" Tygard asked.

I shrugged. "He doesn't want people to know where the photo was taken. Puerto Buena really is a secret hideaway for him."

"Puerto Buena, you said?" Tygard again.

I nodded, placed my drink down, and said, "Now if you'll excuse me, I have some packing to do."

"Going somewhere?" asked Sanders.

I nodded again. "Puerto Buena."

"Peter, what?" cried Jo.

"You shouldn't do that, Mr. Brandt," Tygard said. "It would not be wise."

"Listen to him, Brandt," Sanders said. "Let the professionals handle it."

"Peter!"

"I did that already, Sanders, and he got away."

"Pe-ter!"

"Perhaps, we should go," suggested Tygard.

"I think you're right," replied Sanders. Toward me, he muttered, "Better put on your waders, Brandt. There's going to be a fucking shit storm in here."

As soon as the door closed behind them, I got on the phone to my travel agent. "Megan? Peter Brandt. I need to book a flight to Costa Rica." I glanced up and found Jo glaring at me with a frigid stare. "When? Like yesterday. Yeah, into Juan Santamaría International. Okay, flying from Lindbergh Field." I glanced at my watch. "Plenty of time. Thanks."

Hanging up, I looked at Jo again. She still glared at me but said nothing. "What?" She still said nothing, so I went into the bedroom. Like most journalists who travel a lot, I always kept a go-bag in my closet, a small duffel packed with a change or two of clothes, comfortable boots and, of course, my passport. I grabbed it and stomped into the living room.

"Will you take care of Jack?"

"What are you doing, Peter?" Jo said, her eyes still icy but her voice soft, almost pleading. "After everything we've been discussing about us—about you and me?"

Exasperated, I dropped the bag and faced her. "What do you want me to do, Jo? Just sit here and let Bradwell get away with everything he's done? Could you do that? Did you sit back and do nothing after your men were killed by friendly fire in Desert Storm? No. After recovering from your wound, you went after the people responsible. Right? Admit it, that's what you did."

"But—"

"No, buts, Jo," I told her. "I want Bradwell to pay—not only for killing Keith, but for what Keith's death did to my parents, to me. None of us were the same after that, especially my parents. I can't help believing if Keith lived, they never would have been killed in that car crash. Maybe I wouldn't have run off to Salvador and Nicaragua, never have gotten this." I pointed to the scar running down my forehead and left eye. "Maybe Rhonda would've had a happier life. I don't know, but I can't sit here and wait for something to happen. I love you, Jo, but I can't do nothing."

The frost melted from her stare, replaced by silent tears. I put my arms around her and softened my voice. "Don't worry, Jo, I won't do anything stupid, I promise," I said. "I only want to make sure Bradwell gets caught and is brought back here."

She looked down at the floor. Lifting her chin, I kissed her softly, then more deeply, and she reciprocated. "Now, will you take care of Jack, or do I need to call Cindy?"

"Don't you dare," she whispered, wiping a tear from beneath her eye.

"Thank you." Jack noisily crunched kibble in the kitchen. I picked him up and petted his fur, then took him over to Jo. "All right, big guy, I'm counting on you to keep Jo safe." I kissed him on the head, handed him to Jo, and kissed her head. Picking up my bag, I gave them one last glance and left.

Chapter 31

LINDBERGH FIELD, SAN DIEGO'S international airport, sits on an expanse of reclaimed land mostly dredged
from the bottom of San Diego Bay. It lies a little above sea
level near to Harbor Island, also dredged up from the sea
floor, and where Rhonda and TD met their ends. Coastal
bluffs surround the airport on three sides, meaning Lindbergh sits at the bottom of a geological "soup bowl." That,
and the skyscrapers lining its approach, make it one of the
world's most difficult airports to land in. Former Navy avi-
ators-turned-airline pilots compare flying into San Diego to
landing a jumbo jet on an aircraft carrier.

The airport's name honors Charles Lindbergh for his
flight across the Atlantic in the Spirit of St. Louis, which,
coincidently, was designed, built, and tested in San Diego
close to where the airport sits. The "Lone Eagle" is often

mistakenly credited with piloting the first trans-Atlantic flight in 1927. Yet, sitting in the U.S. Coast Guard base across the street from the airport is a statue of the man who *did* pilot that first crossing, Commander Elmer Stone. Stone, the first Coast Guard aviator, piloted the NC-4, one of four wood-and-fabric, dual-winged Navy seaplanes that set out in 1919 to cross the Atlantic from Newfoundland to Portugal. Only Stone's plane made it all the way. Though the first successful trans-Atlantic flight, it wasn't nonstop. That milestone occurred a few weeks later with a modified Vickers bomber flown by two Royal Air Force pilots. Nor did Stone make his flight alone; there were two Navy aviators with him. All those men risked their lives to push the boundaries of aviation and to bring prestige to their respective countries.

Lindbergh's crossing in the all-metal monoplane, Spirit of St. Louis, was the first *solo* nonstop trans-Atlantic flight, and he did it for money—twenty-five thousand dollars offered to the first person to cross that ocean alone. For his accomplishment, the U.S. presented Lindbergh the Medal of Honor—usually reserved for honoring heroics in combat—and he got bumped up in his Army reserve rank from captain to lieutenant colonel. And those who crossed the Atlantic in rickety wood-and-fabric biplanes nearly ten years before Lindbergh? Largely forgotten to history.

I thought about those forgotten aviators while I stared out the massive glass walls of the concourse, watching the delicate metallic ballet taking place on the airfield—the great flying machines moving about in their orchestrated dance of takeoffs and landings, taxiing and boarding. It was dark outside, and the strobing airport beacon and flashing navigation lights stabbed across the shadowy stage while the metronome-like swing of the ground crews' glowing, orange, marshaling wands directed the lumbering behemoths of the air into their assigned positions on the stage.

Yeah, well, I think like that when I feel morose.

I left the bungalow with more than enough time to make my flight. I didn't want to hang around with the chance Jo would change her mind—or make me change mine. A lingering drink in an airport lounge and I still had time on my hands. Time to think and to regret thinking. Time to stare out of the window and ponder all of life's injustices. Time to waste feeling sorry for myself.

Engrossed with the production outside, I didn't look around when someone with a small roller bag took the seat next to me. I wouldn't have paid the person any attention except that damn bag struck me in the shin not once, but twice. I turned to glare at the intruder.

"Hello, Peter." Jo grinned at me with that delicious, crooked smirk of hers.

"Jo, what are you doing here?"

"Protecting my investment," she said, then corrected herself. "*Our* investment."

"You're going to Costa Rica with me?" I asked. She nodded. I stared at her, my mouth working silently like a fish out of water. My thoughts collided with one another. Happy she would be with me. Afraid she would be with me if things went bad. Finally, I said, "How'd you know which flight I'd be on?"

"You're not the only one with a travel agent, Peter," she said. "But this *is* the only flight going out of Lindbergh tonight with a connection to Costa Rica."

Of course, Jo the cop.

"But … but …" I stuttered. Then I asked, "But who's taking care of Jack?"

"Oh, he'll be fine," she said. "Cindy's taking care of him."

If nothing shocked me yet, that sure did. "You talked to Cindy?" She smiled slyly. "But you hate Cindy."

"She's not so bad after all," Jo said, still with that sly smile. "In fact, we had quite a few laughs comparing notes."

"Comparing notes about what?" Seriously, I didn't think I wanted to know.

"Not what, *who*," she said, and laughed out loud. "If you could only see your face. Now kiss me or I'll tell you *exactly* what we talked about."

Like I said, I really didn't want to know, so I kissed her.

The flight to Juan Santamaria International Airport, situated outside Costa Rica's capital, San Jose, took five hours, not counting the layover in Mexico City. We came off the plane red-eyed, bedraggled, and bone tired—and we still had another flight to the country's east coast. While waiting for that flight, we each washed up a little in the restrooms. By the time we finished, I looked somewhat more presentable, but Jo looked spectacular with her hair brushed out, her makeup refreshened, and her eyes bright.

"It's all makeup and eye drops," she explained, stifling a yawn.

The flight east was much shorter, and the plane much smaller—one of those ubiquitous "puddle jumpers" flown by daredevil pilots across the globe into places where real airliners dare not go. Puerto Buena's airport raised the pucker factor of even those adventurous aviators, being little more than a packed-earth runway with a windsock. Yet, it accommodated the tourists who came to fish, surf, or wonder at the wildlife reserve surrounding the town, most of whom stayed at one of the few resorts allowed in the area. The town itself was little more than a handful of homes, shops, restaurants, and one bar—Te Mana—sitting on a grid of dirt roads. A small bay offered shelter to a dock lined with deep-sea charter boats, many of questionable seaworthiness, and to the small clinker-built wooden fishing boats hauled up on the beach. We had reservations for a room in a small pensione, and I looked forward to a bath and a change of clothes when two men accosted us—one tall, one short, and both wearing the uniform of the local police.

"Señor Brandt?" the short one asked. "Señor Peter Brandt?"

"*Sí*," I replied.

The policemen switched to English. "May I see your passport, please?"

I handed over my passport and asked, also in English, "Is there a problem?"

The officer glanced at my name and photo, then closed the passport. "You will come with us, please," he said. I started to protest, but the taller policeman moved in behind me. "You will come with us, please," the first repeated.

"Wait," Jo said. "What about me?"

"You two are traveling together?" the cop asked. Jo nodded. "Passport, please." She handed him her passport and, again, he glanced inside, then closed it. "You will come with us as well, please."

"Where are we going?" I demanded.

"To our station," the officer said.

"For what?"

"Questioning," he said.

"About what?" I asked.

The policeman smirked. "About whatever the man who wishes to question you asks."

Chapter 32

THE ONE-STORY FAUX adobe Puerto Buena police station stood alone at the edge of the wildlife preserve. Two white patrol cars parked outside wore standard *Policia* markings on the doors. One light-blue sedan sported a gold badge on its door and the large letters OIJ, followed by *Organismo de Investigación Judicial* in smaller letters.

"What does that mean?" asked Jo when I pointed it out to her.

"National criminal police," I said. "Kind of like the FBI."

We parked in front of the station and the two policemen escorted us inside. An officer sat behind the counter in the front lobby, pulling triple duty as watch sergeant, dispatcher, and greeter. Only he didn't greet us. He barely acknowledged our arrival.

The shorter of the two officers, still holding our passports, told us to wait with his friend while he passed through a low swinging door and disappeared down a hallway. Five minutes later he returned and beckoned us to follow him. Without a word, he led us to a door, opened it, ushered us inside, then closed it behind us.

He left us in a small conference room with no windows and a table in the center surrounded by six chairs. A large mirror dominated the far end of the room, which I assumed was one-way glass. The conference room probably doubled as the station's interrogation room.

A man with a wallet badge hanging from the breast pocket of his light beige suit sat at the end of the table below the mirror. He stood about five-nine, considerably well-built for a man I guessed to be in his late forties. His round, tawny face featured a wide smile with brilliant, white teeth. Dark, curly hair topped it all off.

"Ah, Señor Brandt and—" Both of our passports sat on the table in front of him and he glanced at Jo's. "And the beautiful Señorita Rice. Welcome and thank you for coming."

"It's not like we were offered a choice," I said.

The smile disappeared, replaced by a look of concern. "The officers, were they not polite? If they were rude or abusive, I will see them punished."

I shook my head. "They were just … insistent."

"Oh, I understand. In that case, please accept my apologies." The smile returned. "Please sit down then. May I get you anything? Water? Coffee?"

As far as police rousts go, this was the politest I'd ever endured. Jo and I shook our heads and sat down. Despite the politeness and wide smile, our host's eyes remained watchful, as if studying each of us.

"My name is Rubén Moreno," he said. "I am an agent with the OIJ. You know of it?"

"National police," I said.

"Oh, you visited Costa Rica before?" he asked.

"I'm a journalist," I answered. "Back in the Eighties, I covered the wars in Nicaragua and El Salvador. Fellow reporters and I would come to Puerto Buena for R&R."

"Ah, yes, the civil wars," he said, frowning. "Terrible. Terrible. Are you aware Costa Rica has had no wars—civil or otherwise—in decades? Not since we abolished the military in 1948."

"That's admirable," I said, impatient. "Agent Moreno, would you please tell us why you had us brought here? Is there a problem?"

"Problem? No, no problem," he said, shaking his head. "No, I brought you here so I could assist you."

"Assist us? In what?" Jo asked.

"In apprehending this Señor Bradwell," Moreno replied. "A terrible man, I understand."

Jo and I glanced at each other but said nothing.

"Perhaps I should explain," Moreno said. "We have a mutual friend. A Señor Tygard."

I fought the impulse to let my jaw drop open. I glanced at the mirror behind Moreno and said, "I don't think I know anyone with that name."

Moreno caught my glance. "Do not worry," he said. "I assure you there is no one in the next room to watch us or listen."

"I still don't recall anyone by that name," I said. "Do you, Jo?"

Jo frowned and shook her head. "No. No one."

Moreno wagged his head. "Yes, yes, of course. He said you would deny knowing him. So, for you to trust me, he told me to tell you that you have—well, he said a 'very dangerous kitty cat.'"

Jo and I looked at each other again. "He knows Tygard," I said. To Moreno I asked, "But how?"

"But that should be obvious," Moreno said. "We both obey the same masters."

This time, my jaw *did* drop. "You're Mossad?"

Moreno shrugged and said, "I do what I can." He laughed and said, "By the looks on your faces, I see you are confused. But let me explain. My father was a Catholic from here, Costa Rica, my mother a Jew from Israel. They met and fell in love while she vacationed in our country. My parents raised me in both religions."

Moreno reached under his shirt and pulled out a necklace holding both a crucifix and a Star of David.

"That must have been confusing," I said.

"Not as much as one might think," the agent said. He shrugged. "Though for me, learning Latin was easier than learning Hebrew."

"Of course," Jo said, as she made a connection. "Rubén, the Spanish form of the Hebrew name Reuben, the first-born son of Jacob in the Old Testament."

Moreno flashed his smile at Jo. "Beautiful *and* well read."

"But how did you get tangled up with Israeli intelligence?" she asked.

"Such an interesting story and one I enjoy telling— though I rarely get the chance to," Moreno said. "When I finished my secondary education, I moved to Israel to study at the University of Tel Aviv. As I held dual citizenship, I felt I should serve in the army there. After my service, I returned to Costa Rica to complete my studies. One day, I happened to meet one of my old university professors visiting from Tel Aviv as a tourist."

"Don't tell me," I said, remembering Tygard's earlier occupation as a professor. "Tygard."

Moreno grinned, tapped his nose with his finger and pointed at me. "*Exactamente!* That's when he recruited me. I help when I can, and when it does not interfere with my other duties."

"Tell me, agent—"

Moreno held up a hand. "Please, Rubén."

"Tell me, *Rubén,*" I said. "You don't happen to spy for the Vatican, too, do you?"

Rubén threw his hands up with a shrug. "What can I say? They never asked me."

With a chuckle, he stood. "Come," he said. "I have made some inquiries. This Nelson Bradwell has a small cottage on the other side of Puerto Buena. I suggest we pay him a visit. *Sí?*"

We stood as he walked to the door and held it open for us. As we passed down the hall toward the entrance, Moreno said, "While I drive, you can tell me about this 'dangerous kitty' of yours. Is it true what Señor Tygard says? That you live with a *león de montaña*—a mountain lion?"

Chapter 33

NELSON BRADWELL'S COSTA RICAN hideaway, a single-story cottage covered in faux adobe, sat nestled beneath a copse of shade trees. Similar homes filled the grove, separated by enough distance and vegetation to give Bradwell the privacy he desired. Moreno led us up to the door and knocked, as if simply paying a friendly visit. Considering what Bradwell did to Danner's boat, I wasn't as sanguine.

We waited.

Moreno knocked again and called out, "Señor Bradwell?"

And we waited some more.

"I'll go around back," I said, trotting off before Moreno could stop me. The little house had no backyard, no garden of tropical plant life, only a narrow area between the house and the trees void of any vegetation. *Like a killing field*, I thought. I glanced through a side window and saw an empty kitchen. A rear window showed the same view from another angle. A second back window looked in on a bedroom with a single, narrow, unmade bed.

I returned to the front door, shaking my head. "Looks pretty empty," I told Moreno.

Moreno knocked once more, then drew an automatic pistol from a waist holster. "Please stand back, *señor y señorita*," he said.

Knowing Bradwell's skill with explosives, Jo and I needed no prodding. As we backed away from the door, it occurred to me I should warn Moreno, but he'd already pressed down on the door lever. He let the door swing open on its own as he stood to the side. "Señor Bradwell, *policia*. OIJ."

Still no reply, and Moreno took a quick peek around the door jamb. With a second quick glance, he entered the doorway, the pistol raised, and swiftly cleared the front room. A few minutes later, he came to the door holstering his weapon, and said, "Please come in. Our bird appears to have, as you say, flown the coup."

Fled was a more appropriate word. Wherever Bradwell went, he left his little hideaway in a rush. The tiny living room was still neat, but the kitchen looked ransacked. Recently used dirty dishes sat unattended in the sink. Cabinet doors stood agape, their contents either missing or pushed aside. Canned goods lay scattered about as if rejected. I picked up several and noted they had all passed their expiration date.

We found the bedroom in a similar mess. The bed sheets were clean, but slept in. A suitcase sat open on the floor, its contents gone. Street shoes and wrinkled slacks and a shirt littered the floor. Three or four empty clothes hangers lay about in front of an open closet. The single bathroom showed signs of recent, hasty use.

"Looks like he was in a hurry," Jo said.

I nodded. "But to go where?" I kicked at the trousers. "I'm guessing these are the clothes he wore on the flight here. But what did he change into?"

"Nothing fancy, I presume," Jo said, shifting through the remaining clothes in the closet. "He left behind anything he would wear for a night on the town—if such a thing exists here." She poked her head into the closet and sniffed. "Mothballs. If he came here regularly, he probably left clothing in the closet and chest of drawers to wear, with mothballs to keep insects away."

"He comes here to fish," I said. "Maybe he changed and went out on a charter boat?"

"Unlikely, señor," Moreno said, reaching into his pocket and removing a cell phone. "But I will call the local station and have them check." After a brief conversation, he put the phone away and said, "A patrolman is heading to the dock to check. Meanwhile, please continue looking around here while I talk to the neighbors."

After Moreno left, Jo and I moved into the living room. Though not as large as Bradwell's home in Orange County, it still had the same masculine décor. Photos of him fishing, quaffing drinks with touristas and locals, backpacking through a forest. After a while, we gave up and sat on the couch.

Jo sighed. "Well, what now, Peter?"

I shook my head and leaned back against the sofa, staring at the ceiling. "I don't know. Maybe …" I sat up and looked around. On the bookcase stood two photos of Bradwell. The first showed him wearing a backpack hiking up a steep jungle trail, grinning at whomever took the picture. The second, also taken in a rain forest, showed him holding a hunting rifle.

I got up, walked over, and scrutinized them. In the second picture, far in the background, sat the familiar mountain cabin. "Where's his backpack?"

Jo still lay back on the sofa, her eyes closed. "What backpack?"

"The one in this photo," I said, showing her. "And where's the rifle?" Jo glanced at the photos, shrugged, and shook her head. "The food strewn about in the kitchen. The clothing missing from the closet. He was loading up a backpack—this backpack." I tapped the photo of him hiking the trail. "He didn't come here to hide in *this* house. He's heading somewhere else."

Moreno returned, shaking his head. "A neighbor heard him drive in late last night and saw him leave early this morning in a Jeep, probably a rental. And the patrolman reports no charter boats have sailed in the last two days."

"Look at this," I said, handing him the photo. "At his home, I saw another photo of that cabin with him standing on its porch with a young girl. Could he have another hideaway here in Costa Rica?"

"I don't know, senor, but…" He took the photograph out of its frame and looked at the back. Then he did the same with the second photo. "*La Guarida del Diablo.*"

"The Devil's Lair?"

"*Sí.* Here, it is written on the back of the photos," Moreno said.

Now Jo got interested. She stood up and peered over Moreno's shoulder. The writing recorded the location and the year, 1992.

"You know this place?" I asked.

Moreno nodded as he handed the photos back. "I do—unfortunately," he said. "The Devil's Lair is not far from here, but close to the border with Nicaragua. Many years ago, it was a popular place for *touristas* to hike to, and for sport hunters, too. But then came the civil war and the

Contras often took refuge in the rainforest around the Lair—illegally, of course. They often fought with the Sandinistas in the nearby jungle. Then after the war, came the narcos. The cartels, they use the area in their smuggling efforts because it is now very isolated."

"Had the cartels come there by 1992?" I asked.

Moreno nodded. "Why?"

"What was Bradwell—still an American federal law enforcement agent back then—doing hiking into the middle of narco territory?"

Moreno shrugged, but Jo caught on.

"Peter, do you think—"

"Bradwell didn't come to Costa Rica to get away from things," I said. "He was meeting with cartel members, no doubt to sell them information on American counter-drug operations."

"This man, Bradwell," Moreno said. "He is a terrible man, no?"

"You have no idea, Rubén," I said. "Bradwell has a long history of selling out to the enemy. Tell me, how do we get to *La Guarida del Diablo*?"

"Señor Peter, you do not want to go there," Moreno said. "It is difficult to get to, and much more difficult to leave."

I placed my hand on Moreno's shoulder. "This man killed my brother, Rubén," I said. "And he tried to kill me. What would you do?"

Moreno pursed his lips and nodded. "Yes, I under-stand," he said, patting my hand. "But you are not prepared to go now. You need rest, equipment, and—" He glanced at Jo. "The proper clothes and boots."

"I packed the proper clothes and boots," I told him. "But yes, Jo will need to buy those."

"I will drive you to your *pensione* then, and you will rest, eat, and buy the *senorita* some proper clothing. I will collect the equipment you will need, and in the morning, I will take you to where the trail begins. *Sí?*"

I glanced at Jo. She nodded. I turned to Moreno. "*Sí*," I said.

Chapter 34

THE NEXT MORNING, MORENO arrived at our *pensione*, but not to drive us to the Devil's Lair trailhead. The previous evening, Jo bought hiking boots, a pair of trail shorts and a shirt, a packable backpacking jacket shell, and a broad-brim hat. I wore the same hiking boots, khaki trousers and shirt, photographer's vest, and boonie hat I'd worn while covering the Central American conflicts. Moreno wore a suit.

"Good morning, *amigos*!" he greeted us. "Are you ready for your grand adventure?"

"We're ready," I said, looking him up and down. "Are you?"

"Oh," he replied, brushing at the suit. "I am afraid I will not be joining you today. *Lo siento.* Duty prevents me from going with you. But I have all the equipment you will need. Come."

He led us to his car with the OIJ emblem and opened the trunk. Inside were two stuffed rucksacks, plus two expandable hiking poles, which I considered a nice touch. I opened each pack and rummaged through the contents—MREs, the U.S. military rations troops often derided as Meals Rejected by Ethiopia, a hiking compass, a small first-aid kit, survival kit, and a fire-starting kit. Each bag also contained a lightweight rain poncho, extra wool socks, flashlight, water filter and sanitizing tablets, and a short, folding machete. Each also held a fully filled internal two-quart water bladder and straw. All in all, it wasn't a bad kit and I told him so.

"*Gracias,* Señor Peter," Moreno said. "The best I could do on short notice." He reached inside the car and withdrew a topographical map, which he spread out on the hood. As he did, a local police Jeep pulled up. The driver got out and handed Moreno the keys. "I have taken the liberty of borrowing one of the station's Jeeps for you to drive," the agent said as he handed me the keys.

"Now, here is where you need to go," Moreno continued, placing a finger on the map. "Not far as the bird flies, but the road is winding and will take you maybe an hour. Here, there is an old—how do you say…?"

"Jeep trail?" I said, squinting at the map.

"Yes, a jeep trail, but no longer useful for any vehicle," he said. "It is no longer maintained and is overgrown and in disrepair. This is why you must walk. The terrain is rough—plenty of ups and downs, some flats, then more ups and downs. Sometimes more ups than downs." He chuckled at his joke. "But seriously, the trail is extremely rough. Are you certain you want to try this?"

"Bradwell's an old man, Rubén," I said. "If he can climb the damn thing, so can I."

"Yes, but … the *señorita*," Moreno said, eyeing Jo. "I could not help but notice she has a small limp. An injury, perhaps?"

"I'm fine," Jo told him a little too brusquely.

"A war wound," I explained. "Jo served in the Army. Operation Desert Storm."

Moreno's eyes widened with admiration. "Beauty, brains, *and* courage," he said. As an aside to me, he added, "A dangerous combination, *señor*." He gave her a toothy smile. "I feel better knowing that. Come, let us load the Jeep."

As we loaded the packs into the Jeep, Moreno ordered the patrolman to wait in his car. He took a plastic carrying case from the trunk and motioned us to follow him to the far side of the Jeep. Placing the case on a seat inside the Jeep, he opened it, revealing two early model Glock 17s with four loaded, fifteen-round magazines.

"We confiscated these from an American yacht that brought them into the country illegally," he said, his voice lowered. "I offer them for you to use—in an emergency, of course."

"Of course," I replied. Taking a quick glance at the patrolman who appeared engrossed in reading something he'd found in the agent's vehicle, I picked up a pistol and worked the action. Jo did the same. We both nodded in approval and replaced the handguns in their case. "Thank you," I said.

"Courtesy of the Mossad," he said, smiling. "And now, duty calls me, and you must be off. *Via con Dios*. Or—as my mother would say—*shalom*."

The road to the trailhead meandered, as Moreno said, through a rainforest that grew thicker the higher we drove up the foothills. At first, we said little, still jet-lagged and sleep deprived. At last, I asked, "So, what do you think of Agent Moreno?"

"He's very handsome," Jo said, with a sidelong glance at me and the hint of a smile. "Beautiful teeth."

"He certainly seems smitten with you," I said. "Should I be jealous?"

"Well," she said, drawing out the word. "Every woman fantasizes about having a Latin lover. They're so ..."

"Latin?"

"I was thinking sexy," Jo said and chuckled. "He *is* accommodating. All the hiking equipment and the pistols …"

"A little too accommodating, don't you think?" I asked.

"You don't trust him?" Jo asked.

"I'm a journalist," I said. "It's my nature not to trust people."

"Apparently, Tygard trusts him."

"I don't particularly trust Tygard either," I said. "I don't trust the Mossad."

"He saved your life twice in just a few months, Peter," Jo reminded me. "You still don't trust him?"

"Just the other day you raised hell with me for letting him talk me into burglarizing Danner's boat," I said.

"Oh, that," Jo said. "I blamed Sanders for that. *Him* I don't trust."

I sighed. "Yeah, me neither."

We turned off the main road onto a jeep trail that went another five miles before petering out. What had once been a parking area where hikers and hunters left their vehicles was now just a patch of empty earth the jungle had yet to consume. I stopped the Jeep and killed the engine.

"You see something missing?" I asked Jo.

"You mean Bradwell's Jeep?" she answered.

"Yeah, if he went up to the Devil's Lair, where's his car?"

We climbed out and looked around. I spotted fresh tire tracks in the dirt and followed them to where they disappeared into the forest. A few yards into the growth, we found Bradwell's Jeep covered with freshly cut tree branches as camouflage.

"He's here," I said, mimicking the little girl from the *Poltergeist* movie. The Jeep was locked and empty. Whatever he'd packed, he took with him. "Let's get our gear."

Returning to the police Jeep, we started hefting on our packs. We each took a Glock and two magazines, loaded one magazine, and slid a round into the chamber before setting the safety. I slipped my Glock and the extra mag into the right cargo pocket of my photog's vest while Jo placed hers in her pack. The hiking poles were the extendable type, and I opened one to its full length. Walking with the stick felt awkward, so I retracted it and hung it on an external loop on my ruck.

Grass, brush, tree limbs and knotted roots had reclaimed the old jeep trail leading up the mountain. A wooden barricade stood across the trail. Now weathered, what remained of its peeling, faded paint revealed the words *Prohibido el Paso*—No Trespassing. I pointed out recent signs of passage to Jo—snapped branches still moist with sap, boot-crushed ground cover, stones rolled or kicked out of their snug muddy habitats. With a final adjustment of our rucks, we stepped off the trailhead and began our trek up the mountain.

Chapter 35

I SWIM IN THE ocean and jog to keep myself in shape. But no exercise prepares you for walking through a jungle with thirty pounds or more on your back. More so when the air is thick with moisture and the miasma of rotting vegetation. Breathing is like sucking air through a straw stuffed with wet cotton. The muggy heat weighed down on us. Sweat soaked our clothes after the first mile and streamed down our faces in little rivulets that drained into our eyes. Humidity prevented the sweat from evaporating and cooling our bodies. The wetness clung to our skin and clothing, adding to the sense of being weighed down.

The trail was, as Moreno warned, a hellish mix of terrain, with steep ascents and wicked slopes. Deep ruts, carved into the trail by tires long ago and camouflaged with jungle detritus deposited by years of tropical downpours, threatened to trip us or turn an ankle at each step. Jo and I used our hiking poles to test the ground before us. The poles also helped keep us on our feet when climbing or descending scree-covered hills.

At Jo's suggestion, we hiked to an army rhythm—walk for fifty minutes, rest for ten. Even resting, the wet air could not satisfy our oxygen cravings. We spoke little, saving our breath for the next fifty minutes of climbing and stumbling. Four miles in, our water ran low. Stopping at a stream, we refilled our water bladders using the filtration pumps Moreno had supplied. As a secondary precaution, we added disinfecting tabs to the water and sweetened it with electrolyte powder to hide the bitterness of the pills and to replenish the minerals we sweated out.

As we trekked on, the exertion started taking a toll on us. Jo's limp became more pronounced, her injured leg obviously bothering her more. My head throbbed where the scar ran from my forehead to the left check. In a sort of delirium, the pain took me back to those jungles in El Salvador and Nicaragua, back to my twenties, a young eager reporter pushing through the bush toward reports of fighting. We journalists tried to travel in groups, sharing the foolish belief that numbers offered protection, that grouping together kept us safe from the atrocities committed by each side. But the land mines and booby traps placed in the jungle by all sides showed no respect for journalists, no matter how prominently we stenciled our vests and jackets with PRESS or TV. A snap beneath your foot might set off a Bouncing Betsy landmine, hurling an explosive charge into the air to detonate at chest level between you and the person behind you. An unseen wire across a trail snagged by a boot could fling an explosive hailstorm of ball bearings from a hidden directional mine. An ambush erupting at a turn in the trail, and we'd be cut down before the assailants realized we were noncombatants.

Land mines, booby traps, ambushes. The words circled in my head like billboards flashing past on a long, empty road. Landmines, booby traps, ambushes. Landmines, booby traps …

Then, what my befuddled brain tried to tell me struck home like a two-by-four upside the head, an old survival lesson learned years ago and forgotten. *Stay off the trails.* Wiping sweat from my eyes, I stared at the ground and spotted the trip wire only inches ahead of Jo. I lunged after her, gripped her pack, and flung her backward onto the ground. She screamed, landing hard on her back, then rolled onto her knees, cursing.

"What the hell did you do that for, Peter?" she demanded.

I squatted next to the trip wire and pointed. My finger traced the wire across the trail from right to left, then to a pull-ring detonator secured to a stake. Taped to the detonator was a blasting cap attached to a length of det cord—a kind of high-speed explosive fuse—which ran to a Claymore directional mine. The mine's deadly speaker-shaped snout imprinted with FRONT TOWARD ENEMY stared back at the trail. Had Jo taken another step, both of us would have been torn apart by hundreds of metal spheres thrown out by its explosive charge.

"My god," Jo gasped. "I—I didn't see it. What is that doing here?"

"Someone doesn't want visitors," I said.

"Do you think Bradwell planted it?"

I shrugged. "Maybe. Who knows?" I squatted and studied the mine. The plastic casing showed age, but not weathering. "Doesn't look like it's been here long. Maybe placed by the narcos. Maybe Bradwell."

"Where would he get a Claymore?" Jo asked, leaning over my shoulder.

"The Contras used them in Nicaragua," I told her. "The U.S. also sold them to dozens of foreign countries. There must be a lot of them on the black market."

"And Bradwell knows the black market."

"Yes, he does," I said. "Can you disarm this thing?"

"Sure," Jo said. "But why?"

"We don't want to leave it for someone else to trip over," I said. "And because we have to come back this way."

Jo nodded. "Good point." She squatted behind the Claymore and carefully removed the det cord from a plug in the side of the mine. Walking to the stake, she separated the trigger device from the blasting cap. "Safe."

"Good," I said. I shrugged off my ruck and rummaged around until I found the folding machete. "We stay off the trail from now on. Whoever placed that mine may have placed others."

"But why would they do that?" Jo asked.

I used my boonie hat to wipe the sweat off my face. "An early warning device, perhaps, to alert anyone in the Devil's Lair of someone coming up the mountain?" I shrugged. "Maybe a fake planted as a warning to people to keep away?"

"It's not a fake," Jo said. She looked at the trail and shook her head.

"What?" I asked.

"I should have seen the damn thing," she said. "I should have been alert for something like that. I was a soldier—it's my training."

"Your war was in the open desert, Jo," I said. "I cut my baby teeth in these jungles, and I forgot the most basic lesson for survival—avoid walking on trails—until just before I saw the wire."

Jo nodded as I leaned down and picked up the Claymore.

"What are you doing?" she asked as I stowed the device into my pack.

"I don't like littering," I replied. As I coiled the det cord, I asked, "You're sure the Claymore won't go off in my ruck?"

"I'm sure," she said. "The C4 charge is stable. Without the det cord or blasting cap, it can't go off. I'm not so sure about the blasting caps, though."

I stopped shoving the coil of det cord into my bag and looked at her. "Are you kidding me?"

"No," Jo said. "Let me carry them." She put her hand out. "Never carry blasting caps with the explosive."

I thought about it for a moment before handing her the caps. "Good advice." I pulled on my pack again, opened the machete, and began hacking a path through the rainforest parallel to the trail.

"Peter," Jo said as she followed me, shaking her head. "Some of the things you do… sometimes you scare me."

"Sometimes I scare myself, Jo," I said.

Chapter 36

HACKING OUR WAY THROUGH the rain forest only worsened our misery. The exertion from swinging machetes increased our oxygen cravings. Arms became leaden, the muscles screaming for O^2. Our progress was slow, needing to stop often to catch our breath and rub life back into our limbs. Climbing and hacking at vegetation taxed us to our limit, and my brain screamed, "The hell with this! Let's get back on the trail."

Finally, we mounted the last hill, and the trail plateaued into a meadow covered with grass and wildflowers. A collection of small log cabins with covered porticos, originally built to look rustic but now looking old and apparently abandoned, stood scattered around the meadow.

"Welcome to the Devil's Lair," I whispered, as we squatted inside the tree line.

Watching from the tree line, we soon realized not all the cabins were uninhabited. At least, one wasn't. Voices filtered across the clearing speaking English—two with Hispanic accents, one with an American accent. They came from a cabin near the center of the meadow. A man stood at the open door with his back toward us—short and squat with dark hair and skin, wearing a light-colored Guayabera shirt. A pistol dangled from his hand.

Jo and I looked at each other. I nodded to the left. Staying within the trees, we circled the meadow until we reached the back of the cabins. As we moved closer to the middle cabin, we heard angry voices through an open window and left the cover of the trees so we could hear them better.

"I've done good by you." I recognized Bradwell's voice.

A Hispanic voice replied, "Not for a long time, *amigo*. I can't make money on a long time ago."

"I told you, I retired," Bradwell said. "I'm not in the know like I used to be."

"And so, you just abandoned your friends?" the other man said. "You couldn't make a little effort? Talk to people you worked with?"

"Once you're out, you're out," Bradwell said. "No one tells you stuff you're not supposed to know."

"All I know is we had a business arrangement," the man said. "And then you disappear. No more contact with your old friends—almost like you're ashamed of us. Isn't that right, Carlos?"

Carlos, the man by the door, chuckled. "*Sí*, Eduardo, ashamed of us. Breaks my little heart." He sniffed loudly and laughed.

"So, why'd you come here, old man?" said Eduardo. "Maybe you were leading the federales to us?"

"Don't be stupid," Bradwell said. "You'd be in prison today if I hadn't warned you about that raid ten years ago."

"Don't call me stupid, you *gringo*," Eduardo hissed, followed by the sound of someone—no doubt Bradwell—being struck. "I rewarded you well for that. What are you doing here *today*?"

"I came up here to hide out for a while, till things cooled down a bit for me," Bradwell said. "I didn't know you were still here."

"Cooled down from what?"

"I killed someone," Bradwell said. "Someone from my past—way in my past. Vietnam. He would have told NCIS what I did when I worked for them there."

"You fool!" Bradwell grunted as Eduardo struck him again. "You came here with the police after you?"

"Nobody knows I'm in Costa Rica," Bradwell said, his voice muffled as if holding a cloth to a bleeding mouth. "I've told nobody about coming here. Nobody followed me up the mountain."

"How do you know?" Eduardo demanded.

"I left a booby trap on the trail, something I acquired years ago and kept in my little house in Puerto Buena," Bradwell said. "If someone followed me, we'd have heard an explosion."

"How clever." Eduardo's voice oozed sarcasm. "Isn't the gringo clever, Carlos?"

"Clever? I don't know," Carlos said, adding with a chuckle, "I'm still trying to mend my little heart."

"What am I going to do with you, old man?" Eduardo said. His footsteps paced the cabin floor. "What to do with you?"

"Just let me be," Bradwell pleaded. "Let me stay in one of the other cabins until things quiet down again, then I'll be off. I've got my own food. I don't need anything from you."

"Be off where, old man?"

"I'm not sure yet. Somewhere," Bradwell said. "I'll figure it out."

"Maybe you shouldn't go anywhere," Eduardo said. "Maybe you should stay here."

"Can I?"

"Sure, you can, old man," Eduardo said. "As long as you want—six feet down. And you can dig your own grave. Carlos, go find a shovel for Señor Bradwell."

Jo and I scooted back into the tree line as Carlos came out and stomped toward another cabin. Shrugging off my pack, I removed the Claymore, det cord, and trip wire.

"What are you doing?" Jo whispered.

"I've got an idea," I said. "Give me the blasting caps."

Jo handed me the caps and I reassembled the booby trap. "Is this right?" I asked when I finished.

"Yes, but—"

"Shhh."

Carlos came back with a shovel and went inside the cabin. I looked around and picked up a fallen branch that still held some leaves, and a second, sturdier branch. "Stay here."

Stooped over, I scuttled past the open window and planted the Claymore with its snout perpendicular to the cabin threshold and placed the leafy branch in front as camouflage. Footsteps neared the door, and I slipped back to the cover of the cabin, but no one came out. Bradwell pleaded with Eduardo, but the narco struck him again. Carlos laughed. I moved back to the mine, inserted the blasting cap, and trailed the det cord out a few feet from the cabin, where I fastened the pull trigger to the stouter branch and placed it into the wet ground. Gripping the trip wire in my left hand, I stood and stepped in front of the portico, pulling out the Glock.

"Bradwell!" I yelled. "Bradwell, it's Peter Brandt. I know you're in there. Come on out."

Carlos stepped out onto the porch. "Who the fucking hell are you?" he demanded.

"My name's Brandt," I said. "I'm after Bradwell. Nothing to do with you."

Eduardo came to the door—tall, well-built, and good-looking in a ruffian sort of way. He looked back inside the cabin. "So, we'd hear an explosion if someone followed you, eh? *Estúpido.*" He came back to the door. "What do you want with the old man?"

"That's between him and me," I said.

"You some kind of cop?" Carlos called out.

"Maybe," I said.

"Show me your badge," Carlos said.

Of course, I had no badge, so I said the only thing I could think of. "I don't need no stinking badges."

Eduardo laughed. "Funny man, you know that, *gringo*?" he said. "You're a very funny man." He nodded to Carlos. "Bring him here."

Carlos stepped out of the door. I raised the Glock. "Stay where you are," I said. "I've no truck with you. Just send out Bradwell."

Carlos looked back at Eduardo, who tipped his head to the left. The short narco nodded once and side stepped to his left, raising his pistol. Eduardo came out the door, his raised pistol pointing at me, and stepped to his right, putting more distance between him and Carlos.

"Put the gun down, *gringo*," Eduardo said. "You can only get one of us. The other will get you."

"Maybe." I shrugged. "Maybe not."

Then I pulled the trip wire.

Chapter 37

WHAT HAPPENED NEXT TOOK milliseconds but seemed to me to take place in slow motion. I yanked the trip wire and threw myself to the ground as Eduardo fired. A bullet whizzed over my head, but I could only hear the blast of the Claymore. A metal hailstorm swept the two narcos off the porch. They didn't even have time to scream.

I stood, my ears ringing. The Glock shook in my outstretched hand as I stepped toward the now pock-marked cabin portico. The bodies of the narcos lay several feet away, surrounded by the tall grass and wildflowers. Portions of their limbs were gone, their torsos little more than bloody pulp. I stared at them without feeling. In another time, I might have gotten sick. But I'd seen much worse before.

Backing away from the scene, something hard nudged me in the back as I reached the cabin door.

"Guess I owe you my thanks," Bradwell said. "But to hell with that. Give me the gun."

I handed the Glock over my shoulder and turned to face him. Blood smeared his face. His nose lay flattened and bent to the side, one eye swollen and purple. "What the fuck are you doing here, Brandt?"

"As I told those two," I said, jerking my head toward the bodies, "looking for you."

Bradwell sneered. "What for, so you can kill me for killing your brother? Revenge, is it?"

"Something like that."

"What happened, Brandt, happened a long time ago," Bradwell said. "What the hell difference will killing me now make? You think it'll bring your brother back? I told you it wasn't a hill worth dying on."

"I thought more along the lines of revenge for my parents as well," I told him. "And Rhonda, his fiancée. And TD."

Bradwell spat bloody phlegm on the deck. "That punk," he said. "That's who you should be pissed at. If not for him, none of this would've happened. No bomb in the girlie bar, no dead brother. Nothing. Even that punk would still be alive."

Behind Bradwell, I glimpsed a quick movement, a flash of a face, a cold blue eye with blonde hair above. *Jo.*

"Blaming others for your actions, Bradwell?" I said. "In psychology, they call that projection."

"Shut up," Bradwell growled.

His reaction told me I'd hit a chord he didn't like. Remembering what Jo's background investigation of him revealed, I pushed harder at it.

"That why the court sealed your divorce records, to hide your wife's allegations against you? What'ya do—beat her up? Wife beaters always blame the wife."

"Shut up!"

"That why you had to leave the force?" I asked. "Too many roughed-up suspects? I bet you blamed them, too. Said they deserved it, too, didn't you?"

Bradwell's face turned crimson as anger consumed him. "I said, shut up, damn you."

Another movement behind him, Jo's Glock nosing its barrel around the corner of the cabin. Bradwell caught my eye movement and made a quick glance over his shoulder. It was enough to let me step close to him, push his gun hand away and slam the palm of my other hand into his already bloodied nose while my fingers clawed at his eyes. He yelped in pain and backed through the door. The gun fired, but the bullet went wild. I kept the pressure on his damaged nose, my fingers stabbing his eye sockets, and backed him deeper into the cabin until we both tumbled over the back of a sofa.

Bradwell's gun clattered on the ground as we rolled off the couch. He fell on top of me, knocking the air out of me, and grabbed at my throat. I reached up with both hands between his arms and jammed my thumbs into his eyes. His head yanked back, allowing me to break his grip on my neck and heave him off of me. I stumbled to my feet, but he kicked out and caught me behind my right knee cap. The knee buckled, and I crumbled to the floor. He clawed for his pistol, found it, and hauled himself to his feet. I watched his finger tighten around the trigger as he aimed at my head.

"Drop it, Bradwell!" Jo hollered in a strong and commanding voice. She stood at the door in a wide, shooting stance, the Glock held in both hands and trained on Bradwell. The blue eyes behind the gun sight were cold and steady. "Drop it!"

Bradwell glanced at her, then me, and tossed the pistol on the couch. "Got a woman fighting your fights, eh, Brandt?" he sneered.

Standing, I grabbed his pistol, and with the strength of twenty-five years of built-up anger and rage over Keith's death, raked the barrel across his face. Pushing him against the cabin wall, I shoved the barrel into his bloody, gaping mouth. "Try something, anything, *something* to give me a reason to blow your goddamn head off!"

The disdain in his eyes disappeared, replaced by a fearful realization that a madman now stood before him.

"Outside," I ordered as I dragged him toward the door.

Jo lowered her pistol and stepped aside, staring at me as we passed her. "Peter?" she said. "Peter, what are you going to do?"

I ignored her, pulling Bradwell by the shirt collar out of the cabin and off the portico to where Eduardo and Carlos lay. Bradwell peered down at the bodies and wretched. Afterward, he wiped his mouth on his sleeve and looked at me, his one good eye pleading.

"Look, I'm sorry about your brother," he whined. "It was an accident. He wasn't even supposed to be there. It wasn't my fault. I needed to kill that punk kid—TD."

"Why'd you kill your own agents?" I demanded.

"I—I had to," he whimpered. "They knew about me and the black market—because of what the goddam kid told them. You see? The kid's fault all along. He started it all."

I aimed the pistol at his good eye, so the barrel looked like a cannon to him.

"Look, I got money, lots of it," Bradwell blurted. "I can make it up to you. All those years you missed your brother. I can make it better for you."

"You think money can make up for killing my brother?" I screamed. "You think this is what it's all about?"

Bradwell's head shook side to side, whether to show he didn't mean what he said or from fear, I couldn't tell, and I didn't care.

"No, no, *please*!" He dropped to his knees in supplication, pleading with me, begging me for salvation. I wanted so much to see his brains splattered across the field, breathe in the blood-scented stench of revenge and vengeance, the culmination of nearly three decades of hurt and loss. All that would disappear if I tightened my finger a little more on the trigger. Just a little tighter …

"Peter."

Jo's voice, quiet and plaintive. Suddenly, the anger vanished.

The arrogant, sociopathic rich kid turned corrupt cop and federal agent, the bastard who murdered my brother and shattered the lives of my parents and Rhonda, and, yes, me, the son of a bitch who killed TD and nearly killed me—that man no longer existed. All I saw before me was a pathetic, frightened old man begging for his life.

Vengeance is mine … saith the Lord.

I decided I would leave vengeance to the Almighty.

Lowering the gun, I turned my back on Nelson Bradwell and walked away. When I reached Jo, I saw relief in her eyes. I wrapped her in my arms and then, still arm-in-arm, we both walked away from him.

But Bradwell's newfound humility didn't last long.

"I knew you couldn't do it, kid," he yelled. "You don't have the guts. You think you're better than me, huh? Well, you're not. Takes a man to kill another man in cold blood. I know. And you ain't no man, are you, Brandt?"

The thought of turning and shooting Bradwell dead flickered through my head, but I was too tired. Too tired of hating, too tired of the violence, too tired of giving a damn. We walked on.

"I bet your brother is real proud of you, Brandt, you pussy," Bradwell screamed, his voice hysterical. "I bet he's turning over in his grave, he's so embarrassed of you. But if he's your brother, he wasn't much of a shit, either. You know that, Brandt? You know—"

A single gunshot drowned out Bradwell's last word.

Jo and I jumped at the sound. Turning, we raised our pistols and gaped. Bradwell lay face down in the grass, his forehead gone, blood and gray pulp from his shattered brain strewn across the colorful flowers.

Behind Bradwell, his pistol still smoking, stood Rubén Moreno.

Chapter 38

"SEÑOR TYGARD," MORENA SAID, "he told me you were not a cold-blooded killer." He shrugged. "I, on the other hand, am."

"What the hell, Moreno?" I yelled. "Why'd you kill him?"

Moreno wore olive-drab fatigue pants and a khaki shirt with cloth epaulets beneath an armored vest. Emblazoned on the vest were the words POLICIA and OIJ. He picked up his spent cartridge.

"Why?" I demanded.

Moreno pocketed the cartridge. "Mossad," he said, with a shrug, "has a long memory."

"What's that supposed to mean?"

Even as I asked, the answer came to me. Tygard in the parking lot of the university library. I asked if he'd ever heard of Nelson Bradwell. *I know of him,* he replied. *From time to time, he has come across our—as you say—our radar screen.*

"Bradwell had run-ins with the Mossad." I said, a statement, not a question. "When? Back when he worked for NCIS in the Middle East?"

Moreno nodded. "In that position, he possessed access to some of our secrets," he said, "which he sold to our enemies. Several of our intelligence assets in Arab countries were exposed and eliminated by our opponents. Our counter-intelligence people provided evidence of his treachery to his superiors, but they refused to believe." He shrugged. "Perhaps they were too embarrassed to believe." He shrugged again. "But they did nothing. Our people considered eliminating the pig at once, but they feared killing him would injure our relations with your country."

"So, you just let him be?" I asked.

"We limited what intelligence we shared with his agency," Moreno said, "until he returned to the United States and became your country's problem."

"So why kill him now?" Jo asked.

"As I said, Mossad has a long memory," Moreno said.

"Revenge," I said, with a sigh. Moreno nodded.

Vengeance is mine ...

"My apologies, but I had hope for you not to witness this," Moreno said. "I tried to discourage you from coming up here. Remember? I told you how dangerous and difficult the climb would be. Honestly, *señor y señorita*, I never expected you to complete the climb."

"And now what?" I demanded. "What about us?"

Moreno's brow knitted in puzzlement. "What about you?"

"Are you going to kill us, too?" I demanded. "You don't want to leave witnesses around, do you?"

Moreno looked genuinely surprised. "Señor Brandt, Mossad has nothing against you two," he said. "Señor Tygard has the highest regard for you. And the *señorita* is much too lovely to kill."

He removed and pocketed the pistol's magazine. Detaching the slide from the frame, he slipped the barrel out and stuck it in his back pocket. From a cargo pocket in his pants, he removed another barrel, which he inserted into the slide, and reassembled the gun. He reloaded and holstered the pistol. The bullet that killed Bradwell would never be traced to Moreno's weapon.

Moreno looked at me, his lips pursed in thought. His cheeks puffed up, and he blew air through his puckered lips. "But you are right," he said. "You two should not be witnesses to all this." He waved his hands at the bodies. "I strongly recommend you return to your *pensione* and make arrangements for your flights back to the States. You go home and you tell whoever you must tell that you came to

Puerto Buena, found the home of this pig—" He spat toward Bradwell's body. "But he had fled from there to—how do you say? Parts unknown. Then you returned home. You never found Bradwell, and you never came here to this mountain. *Comprende?*"

Jo and I nodded. "What about the bodies?" I asked.

Moreno glanced at the dead men and shrugged. "We leave them. Animals have to eat, no?" he said. "In a month or two, maybe three, my department will make another sweep of the area looking for narcos. If there is anything left of them, my officers will assume warring narcos killed each other. It happens that way, *sí?*"

"*Sí,*" I said, nodding.

"Now I suggest you gather your bags and go," Moreno said.

Still stunned, we turned to retrieve our rucksacks. The straps on my ruck snagged on my damp shirt and I snapped out of my fugue.

"Wait a minute, Rubén," I said. "How the hell did you get up here? It took us almost six hours to climb that hill. Look at us—we're sweaty messes. You've barely worked up a sweat."

"Ah! Did I forget to tell you there is another road on the other side of the mountain?" he said. "*Lo siento mucho.* Yes, this road climbs much higher up. Only we and the cartels know about this road, you see."

"You couldn't tell us?" Jo asked. "Why?"

Moreno spread his hands out and shrugged. "Lovely *se-ñorita*, I am a spy. I don't give away secrets—I steal them." Moreno flashed his big, white grin. "However, since you now know, I suppose I can offer you a ride down the mountain to your Jeep. The very least I can do, *sí*?"

"*Sí*," Jo and I said together.

"Well, then, *vamos*!"

The trip down the mountain was uneventful. Moreno dropped us off where we parked the police Jeep, and we followed him back to Puerto Buena. After returning the Jeep to the station, Moreno drove us to our *pensione*. I considered stopping at Te Mana and having a drink for old time's sake, but Moreno was right. We needed to leave town post-haste. Besides, I had enough nightmares for old time's sake, and we'd just added a few more.

We caught the puddle jumper to the international airport and boarded a flight to Mexico City. Jo quickly fell asleep, and I soon followed her. In Mexico City, we switched planes for the flight back to San Diego. Jo remained quiet during the stopover, barely saying a word until we boarded the home-bound plane.

"Peter," she said. "What we did—no, what you did—flying down to Costa Rica, chasing Bradwell up that mountain, the Claymore and the narcos—in the end, was it all necessary?"

I sighed. "No, not in the end."

"Were you also reckless and irresponsible?"

"Yes," I conceded.

"Then why'd you do it all?"

"What Bradwell said—revenge, retribution, whatever," I said. "I wanted to punish him. No, I wanted to *kill* him. I wanted him to suffer. But when it came down to it …" I shrugged. "Like Bradwell said, killing him wouldn't bring back Keith or Rhonda, or anything. Remember what the Bible says about revenge? 'Vengeance is mine … sayeth the Lord.' In the end, I decided to leave it up to God. Who knew Moreno was going to act as the terrible swift sword of God?"

"More like the Mossad's terrible long memory," Jo said. "You're not going to do anything like that again, are you?"

"I hope not," I said.

"Good," Jo said. "Because if you ever do, I swear to God, Peter Brandt, I'll kill you myself."

Epilogue

One Year Later

JACK SAT AT THE front window, pawing the glass and meowing mournfully, trying to get the attention of his two favorite women. Jo and Cindy chatted on the sidewalk while I finished dressing for the event. Jo wore a tasteful red business suit with a white shirt and a ruffled collar. Cindy wore her usual next-to-nothingness, her tanned skin glistening with tanning oil. Now and then they would turn toward the window and giggle. Unfortunately, they were not giggling about Jack.

When we had returned home, we told the story just as Moreno suggested—we tracked Bradwell to his home in Puerto Buena, but he apparently had fled from there, too. With no idea where to look next, we came home. It seemed to satisfy Mike McCarty, who still seemed miffed at me for interfering with *two* of his murder investigations—Rhonda's and Danner's. Dick Sanders accepted our story and so did Tygard, though the look in his eyes told me he knew damn well what really happened in Costa Rica.

Jack kept pawing at the glass, his way of telling the ladies he wanted them to come in and fawn over him. They both glanced at the window, saw me standing next to Jack and waved, which elicited more giggles.

"Jack," I sighed, "you don't know when you have it well off."

I slipped on my sports jacket and adjusted my tie. "Jo and I will be back in a few hours, Jack. You've got lots of kibble, and I cleaned your box. Count your blessings you're not me going out there."

I stepped out of the bungalow and walked to my Mustang. Cindy waved to me and said, "Hi, there, Professor Pete."

"Hi, Cindy," I said. To Jo, I raised my left arm and pointed to my watch. "We gotta go, Jo."

"Coming, Professor Pete," she said, which started another round of girlish giggles at my expense.

We took SeaWorld Drive out of Ocean Beach to the I-5 freeway and headed north. Getting off at La Jolla, we drove up Mount Soledad to the Veterans' Memorial, where I'd met with Colonel Candee a year before. It was Veteran's

Day, and as usual there would be an event honoring local men and women who had served. New veterans' plaques were to be unveiled, and one in particular brought us up the mountain.

It took a lot of finagling and some questionable "service documents" provided courtesy of Tygard—not to mention a healthy donation—but our plaque finally received approval. Jo and I wended our way through the crowd, but the throng made finding the plaque difficult. In time, I spotted Aaron Lemieux. He hung onto Colonel Candee with his remaining arm, tears streaming down his face. I had invited Lemieux, his friend Scott Alexander, and the colonel to the unveiling. Only Lemieux and Candee could attend; Alexander was in hospice care, soon to be the latest victim of the Vietnam War.

Shortly after returning from Costa Rica, I'd called all three men to explain how Keith and TD died. Facing exposure of his black-market crimes, I told them, the NIS agent, Bradwell, planted two bombs in the Saigon dive to kill TD and two of his own agents. Keith was an innocent bystander who rushed back into the bar after the first explosion to rescue his friend. I didn't tell them how TD survived the blasts or what he'd become afterward. As far as they were concerned, TD died along with Keith.

We made our way over to them, and I introduced Jo. Embarrassed, Lemieux tried wiping the tears from his eyes with his one hand. Then he draped that heavy remaining arm across my shoulders and, looking at the plaque, nodded and said, "You done your brother proud, Pete. TD, too. All of them."

The plaque stood out from the others, each of which honored only an individual veteran. Keith's plaque featured the photograph of him, TD, and Rhonda, all three young, happy, and smiling. Above the photo was a simple legend reading:

KEITH BRANT

RHONDA WHITE

THOMAS DYKSTRA

USMC

KIA 1972 VIETNAM

Of course, only Keith died that day in Vietnam, but the lives of TD and Rhonda ended, too. The lives they lived after that day were lives hardly worth living, Tommy living on the run while Rhonda became a shriveled, empty shell of the once vibrant, young woman she had been. They were victims as much as Keith and, in my mind, Keith got the better deal.

As the ceremony ended, the crowd melted away. Soon, Lemieux and Colonel Candee drifted away, leaving Jo and me to stare at the plaque. I placed my hand on the photo, lowered my head, and said goodbye to my brother one last time. Then Jo took my hand, and we slowly walked away.

THIS IS A WORK of fiction, though many of the background details are factual. Black marketeering during the Vietnam War was rampant, worse than that seen in any earlier war. Decades after the North's victory over the South, Saigon—renamed Ho Chi Minh City—continued to be the hub of the Southeast Asia black market. In 1972, after beginning a withdrawal from the conflict, the United States had to rush squadrons of combat aircraft back into South Vietnam to help hold back the North's Easter Offensive. Ground troops followed to protect the air squadrons from attacks by Viet Cong and North Vietnamese Army ground forces. Once again, the U.S. took more casualties. And as with the fictional character Scott Alexander, Agent Orange exposure continued to plague Vietnam veterans for decades after the war. Ultimately, thousands more service members

who survived the fighting died years later from Agent Or-
ange-related illnesses than there were troops killed in action
during the entire war.

About the Author

MARTIN ROY HILL is the author of two national award-winning series—the Linus Schag, NCIS, thrillers and the Peter Brandt mysteries—as well as the USCG DSF-Papa sci-fi thrillers, the national award-winning WWII thriller, *Codename: Parsifal, Eden: A Sci-Fi Novella*, and a collection of short stories, *DUTY*. He is a former journalist and national award-winning investigative reporter for newspapers and magazines. His nonfiction work has appeared in *Reader's Digest, LIFE, Newsweek, Omni*, the *Los Angeles Times*, and many others. His short fiction has appeared in *Alfred Hitchcock Mystery Magazine, ALT HIST: The Journal of Historical Fiction and Alternate History, Nebula Rift, Mystery Weekly, Crimson Streets*, and others.

He lives in San Diego, California, with his wife, Winke, son, Brandon, and their three feline overlords.

You can follow Martin Roy Hill on social media, buy his books, or visit his website by going to this link: https://linktr.ee/martinroyhill

If you enjoyed reading this book, please leave a review on Amazon.com, Barnes & Noble, Goodreads, or your favorite review site.